I0599396

THE DEW OF HEAVEN

OTHER BOOKS IN THE ARGOSY LIBRARY:

SATAN'S LASH: THE COMPLETE CASES
OF SATAN HALL, VOLUME 1
CARROLL JOHN DALY

THE ROSE BATH RIDDLE: THE COMPLETE
CASES OF JIGGER MASTERS, VOLUME 2
ANTHONY RUD

EAST OF SUEZ
THEODORE ROSCOE

GOLDEN DERRINGERS
J.E. GRINSTEAD

THE DUCHESS PULLS A FAST ONE: THE
COMPLETE CASES OF THE DUCHESS
WHITMAN CHAMBERS

THE INVASION OF AMERICA
FREDERICK C. PAINTON

BAIT FOR MEN: THE COMPLETE CASES
OF THE LADY FROM HELL, VOLUME 1
EUGENE THOMAS

THE FESTIVAL OF THE DEAD: THE
COMPLETE CHINATOWN CASES OF
JIMMY WENTWORTH, VOLUME 1
SIDNEY HERSCHEL SMALL

BEYOND THE LAW
J. ALLAN DUNN

THE DEW OF HEAVEN

MAX BRAND

ILLUSTRATED BY
SAMUEL CAHAN

COVER BY
PAUL STAHR

POPULAR PUBLICATIONS · 2022

© 2022 Popular Publications, an imprint of Steeger Properties, LLC

First Edition—2022

PUBLISHING HISTORY

"The Dew of Heaven" originally appeared in the September 7–October 12, 1935
    issues of *Argosy* magazine (Vol. 258, No. 3–Vol. 259, No. 2). Copyright © 1935
    by The Frank A. Munsey Company. Copyright renewed © 1962 and assigned to
    the Frederick Faust Family Trust. All rights reserved. Images copyright © 1935
    by The Frank A. Munsey Company. Copyright renewed © 1962 and assigned to
    Steeger Properties, LLC. All rights reserved.

ALL RIGHTS RESERVED

No part of this book may be reproduced or utilized in any form or by any means
    without permission in writing from the publisher.

Visit argosymagazine.com for more books like this.

TABLE OF CONTENTS

THE DEW OF HEAVEN

THE DEW OF HEAVEN

Blood ran as freely as gold on the Spanish
Main in the days of Tranquillo the pirate

1

BUCCANEERS ABOARD

THE SETTING MOON dipped its chin in gold and puffed its cheeks. It was not the golden stain on the moon but the green along the horizon that told Ivor Kildare the sun was of about to rise over the Caribbean Sea. The wind was almost dead and the boat felt no waves at all, though the eye could see bright and dark lines running over the water.

Kildare, looking aft into the south-west, studied the triangular sail which had been looming there for some time; and now, as the light of dawn girdled the sea more brightly, he could make out the topsails of a large ship.

Her lofty masts still could catch a breeze, but the low triangle of canvas on the smaller boat behind could reach little higher than Kildare's own small craft. That meant oars.

And every ship, great or small, meant danger. It might be that Henry Morgan had sent out a swift periagua loaded with picked men to try to overhaul the fugitives, and perhaps the tall ship behind was another craft loaded with buccaneers, still drunk after the sacking of the city.

He turned to the Indian who stood by the mast, erect, silent, watching the same sail which troubled Kildare. The moonlight gilded his naked body from hips to head and repainted the shadows to make his strength seem greater.

Kildare looked down at his left hand, bandaged but still frightfully hurt by the sword blade which he had grasped in the naked fingers not many days before.

His own broken sword, no longer than a dagger blade now, remained driven into the bow of the periagua, where the hilt of it stood up against the lighted sea to make a dark little cross.

"Luck, or bad luck, Luis," said Kildare to the tall Mosquito Indian who had followed him with such a perfect devotion through so many dangers.

"My heart tells me nothing, father," said the Indian; and Kildare went on forward. He leaned over the girl who lay fast asleep. As he bent lower, in her sleep she smiled. Her hair in the morning light made a pool of brightness

*It was murder,
not battle*

about her face; and a curious pain ran through the heart of Kildare.

She had wakened, but without moving hand or head she kept on smiling while her eyes drifted over his face.

"Is there trouble?" she asked.

"There is a sail behind us, and every sail means trouble."

She stood up. As she peered over the sea through the dazzle of the sunrise, her hands were busy arranging her hair, and all he could watch was the slender fingers and the movements of the wrists. He felt like a low-born thief that has stolen the emperor's favorite hawk, or has slipped away with the noblest horse in a king's wide pastures. She, like a poor, mute, senseless thing, accepted him as though he were himself the king.

"They are gaining on us, Ivor," she said. "But why should every sail be an enemy?"

"It is likely that the sail either comes from Captain Morgan's fleet or that it is a Spaniard. Henry Morgan will hang me because he knows that I am Ivor Kildare. The Spaniards will hang me because they still think that I am Captain Tranquillo."

INSTEAD OF ANSWERING him directly, she said thoughtfully:

"He was a very famous pirate, that Tranquillo."

"He is a very dead pirate now," replied Kildare.

"If they are Spaniards," she said, "they will listen to me because my name is Heredia, and because the uncle of Ines Heredia is that rich and famous Larretta. Why, Ivor, they would be more likely to cherish you for the sake of the greater reward they will get if they turn me over to my uncle. Besides, they might not recognize you as the man who was captured and taken to Porto Bello."

"You have a reasonable way of speaking," said Kildare. "Do you believe all this in your heart?"

She took a breath and shook her head a little, as people do when they wish to get tears from their eyes. The sun came up that moment and drowned the world with brilliance. It seemed to Kildare that every eye within a hundred miles must see her, she was so beautiful. She interlaced her fingers. Her lips stirred a little.

"Prayers won't turn Spaniards into Englishmen," he told her. "Better pray for a wind, Ines; or shall I whistle for one?"

She had to draw her thoughts away from her prayers

and from the sight of that triangular sail behind them, which was now turning from blue to white. "Do I love you because you are so brave, or because you are such a wild-headed hawk?" she asked, smiling at him.

"You love me for a cheaper reason than that."

"What is the reason, then?"

"Because I am yours. Ines, Ines, please don't cry. This may be our last hour on earth together. Don't spoil it with tears."

"I won't," she answered. "You ought to know, being so wise, that when a woman's eyes are wet she is often farthest from weeping."

He took her in his arms and kissed her again and again.

"That is the last. That is our farewell," he told her.

"Look, Ivor! There comes the wind, darkening the sea!"

"Only a puff," he answered. "And see that fellow walk up behind us with his sweeps. That's a true periagua made all of one cedar tree—and twenty men, at least, manning it."

The big oars flashed. They could make out the craft clearly now, and see its sharpness at either end. It had the grace of an Indian's workmanship, but already they could see that white men were at the oars, and standing in the stern was a fellow whose hair darkened and brightened in the wind like metal gold.

"Aye," said Kildare. "Morgan's men!"

"God will not give us back to that beast, Ivor!"

"Those are buccaneers; and the buccaneers have gathered from the whole Caribbean to follow Henry Morgan."

"How can you tell that they are buccaneers?"

"Do you see those fellows in the bows with the long muskets? That is the buccaneer way, and even at this distance every one of them could shoot his man through the head. See the dark of their bodies, too. They've made free with sun that would have killed most Europeans. But I tell them by those wide hats and the peaked crowns. If you want more—see that winking of light at the masthead. That's a machete tied there for a flag!"

A NEGRO VOICE rose in a husky wail that broke and fell and rose again.

"Aye, buccaneers," said Kildare. "Every man of the lot has been drunk many a time in Tortuga, I'll swear; and they've killed cattle and buccaned the meat in the woods of Hispaniola. They have to have a slave sing for them or they won't enjoy rowing even if there's a treasure at the other end of the cruise."

"Ivor, there is something that can be done!"

"We can open the sky and climb up on a ladder of sunbeams. There's no other way. In the meantime, a little fighting. Ines, lie flat in the bottom of the boat—there by the mast!"

He picked up a pair of the muskets which were in the stern and, dropping to his knees, held the guns in view at the length of his arms. Luis, the Indian, already was aiming a gun.

"Holla! Holla!" he called.

"Holla!" came the hail from the periagua. "Tranquillo! Ho, Captain Tranquillo! We are coming on board you!"

Kildare watched the steady springing of the crystal wave at the bow of the periagua. He saw the sun-blackened faces of the rowers who, still at their work, turned and regarded him over their naked, powerful shoulders. He was aware, not for the first time in his life, of his own slenderness; a cat among fighting dogs.

"Come, my friends, and welcome!" called Kildare. "I have guns here and they are ready for you."

The tall man with the blowing golden hair took off his hat and raised it high above his head. Such a figure never had been seen before, surely, in such company. He wore a dove-colored blouse buttoned with gold, a lace collar, and more lace falling gracefully over his wrists, an absurd little blue jacket came hardly halfway to his belt.

"Madame, and Captain Tranquillo," he called. "We are in fact your friends—but—backwater and keep your distance, lads."

The sea gurgled from blue to green around the big sweeps as they were thrust at a sharp angle down into the water. The periagua lost its way almost at once. One of the men in the bows spat tobacco juice over the side and growled, "Slap him in the face with a quid of lead and he'll listen with his mind open, Louis."

"It is Louis d'Or!" whispered the girl. She had not stretched herself in the bottom of the boat as he suggested. She was just behind him, standing as straight as any man.

Some men said that Captain Louis d'Or was a renegade noble from the court of Louis XIV. His reputation, however, was as red as that of Henry Morgan or any other throat-cutter of them all. The beauty of his face, the elegance of his clothes and manner, simply made him more horrible to the mind. His buccaneers had trailed their oars and picked up enough guns to blow the little craft of Kildare out of the water; but Louis d'Or remained in the stern of the boat, quite unafraid.

HE CALLED OUT, "You see, Tranquillo, that we must board

you. Are you going to die fighting, like a fool, or live a while like a wise man?"

"There is the lady," said Kildare.

"Ah, damn the lady, and damn the talking, too!" bawled a great voice. "Close with him, Louis!"

"If that's the bargain, Tranquillo, I make it gladly," said the Frenchman. "After all, she's not rum that can be poured into twenty cups."

"You have a cross-hilted dagger in your belt," said Kildare. "Swear on it."

"To hell with this fol-de-rol!" yelled a buccaneer. "Let's take the boat." He stood up above the side of the periagua with a machete in his left hand and a pistol in his right. But a companion caught him by the long hair and pulled back his head.

"If we can buy him for a word or two, why should we pay three or four lives? That is Tranquillo, blockhead!"

"A lucky thought of yours," said Louis d'Or, in the meantime. He drew out the dagger. A red stone gleamed like fire in the heel of the pommel. "I swear never to touch the lady; never to allow another man to touch her, Tranquillo—except with permission."

He laughed as he ended his oath and jammed the dagger home in its sheath. "Close in. Lay her alongside; give way on the right. That's enough. I'll board her alone, because something may be broken in a rush!"

The periagua slid alongside and touched the small boat with a singular delicacy. Captain Louis d'Or stepped on board and at once jerked up the tarpaulin on which the girl had been sleeping in the bows. Turning, he scanned the nakedness of the hull.

"It's not in sight," said Louis. "You can tell me where it is, Tranquillo. What have you done with the treasure of the Santa Cruce?"

"I never heard of it," said Kildare.

"You never heard of the great galleon that other Tranquillo captured?"

"Never."

"You knew nothing of the way he gave the gold and silver she carried to his men and only kept for himself a double handful of emeralds and rubies and diamonds?"

"I knew nothing of that."

"You thought he was almost a poor man?"

"Yes."

"Tranquillo the Second, or whoever you are, in the name of God why do you expect me to believe that?"

"The truth ought to be seen, Louis d'Or."

"And you trailed Tranquillo across the Caribbean just for the pleasure of stabbing him when you found him?"

"No, I was the man who ran, and he was the man who followed."

"Ah?" said Louis d'Or. "Swarm aboard, lads. Tie Tranquillo like a goat for the market. Pitch him and the girl into the periagua—and then help me search this boat."

The twenty or more buccaneers had been waiting with glistening eyes, pulling at their mustaches, held perfectly silent by their interest. Now they rose in a brown wave and washed on board the smaller boat.

2

WHITE MAGIC

THEY TIED KILDARE not with cruel force but securely, like men who knew their business, and then followed orders precisely by throwing him headlong into the stern of the long craft.

He turned his head, in midair, to keep from cracking his skull against a crosspiece, made his body limp, and landed without the least injury. The girl came swiftly, without a cry, and leaned over him. The Indian, writhing against the ropes that held him, could do nothing.

"Nothing," said Kildare. "They didn't even bruise the ninth of my lives."

Several of the buccaneers had remained, uninstructed, in the periagua. One of them stood over the prisoner and the girl, and spoke in the garbled Spanish which served all the Finns and Germans and English and French and Italians and Russians who buccaned meat in Hispaniola and who called themselves—because she was the strong nation on the sea—English. In this tongue he said, "I thought you were a man and a captain, Tranquillo. But you're no bigger than a child. There's no room inside your ribs for a heart. Girl, don't touch his ropes!"

He lifted the weight of his hand, but when she took her

touch from the arm of Kildare and watched the big fellow, quietly, he let his hand fall again.

The human tide came pouring back into the periagua.

"Pick up Tranquillo," commanded Louis d'Or.

The big man who guarded the prisoner obeyed by gripping Kildare by the hair of his head and jerking him to his feet. And then with a start of savage pleasure the brute stared; but no sound had come from Kildare.

Tall Louis d'Or, walking aft, confronted Kildare with, "What did you do with it?"

"That treasure you talk about? I've never touched it."

"You said more than that. You never had heard of it, either."

Kildare watched the sneer in the face of the Frenchman. "I never heard of it."

"That's the lie of a fool," said Louis d'Or. "Look here!"

He pointed to the side of the periagua. Over a squared bit of surface the cedar had been trimmed flat and rubbed smooth, and into the wood had been cut a number of little rude pictures such as a sailor knows how to make with his knife—a church with a spindling cross above it, a gallows, three conventional trees for a forest, a long rapier, a sloop under sail, and the most ambitious design of all: a forested mountain with the sun rising over its head. But the carving of hands seemed to be the chief pleasure of the artist. A dozen or more of them were clearly drawn. Between the scattered figures, words which had no connection with one another were worked into the wood with the edge of the knife. On the whole it was rather delicate work.

"This was the favorite boat of Captain Tranquillo the First," said Louis d'Or. "But you know that as well as I know it. And when he sat here at the tiller he filled up some of the hot hours at sea whittling away at this damned, silly cipher. It's a message. About what? About his treasure— which you trailed till you found Tranquillo the Second. Except that he had treasure to write about, why would he have put this work into a bit of wood no bigger than my two hands?"

"He may have had enough jewels to break the back of a Spanish mule," said Kildare. "But about that I know nothing. I give you my word—"

"You will give me plenty of words before I'm done with you. Fetch him to the mast, my lads!" said Louis d'Or. "No, wait for a moment. Read off what's written here, and that may buy you a chance for a little more quiet, Tranquillo."

"I can read the words," said Kildare, "but I can't put a meaning into them unless I have a chance to study them."

"Study 'em at the masthead!" said one of the crew.

They dragged Kildare forward. He gave one look to the girl and saw that she had sunk to the bottom of the periagua and stared hopelessly down.

"Rig a tackle at the masthead," commanded Louis d'Or. "Briskly, now."

ONE OF THE buccaneers ran up the mast like a monkey with a tarry rope end gripped in his teeth. In a moment he was down again with the rope passed through the block above.

"Free his legs so he can dance," said Louis d'Or. "Tie his hands behind his back and fasten the line to them.— Now, Tranquillo, you see how you stand. The line's taut. A word from me and up you go into the air. You know what will happen then. Your muscles and tendons will hold for a while, but in a bit they'll give way. Your shoulders will break from in back. You'll never lift hand again while you live."

"I know those things," said Kildare.

He looked up, not in hope but because it was necessary to take a deep breath.

"So I ask you again," said Louis d'Or. "What do you know of the treasure of Tranquillo?"

"I've been through the hands of Henry Morgan," said Kildare. "Isn't that the sieve to catch big jewels or small ones? If I'd carried anything away, it would be in the small boat, there, and you've found nothing. Or if I knew anything, Louis d'Or, what a fool I would be to pay with my life—aye, or with the use of my arms—for the sake of keeping a few handfuls of treasure!"

"You talk well enough, but you talk about the wrong things," said Louis d'Or. "Up with him, lads!"

The Indian made a vain effort to break from his ropes and help Kildare.

Louis d'Or had stepped back and was raising his hand when such a cry came from Ines Heredia that even through the sweating flesh of those half-naked brutes ran a shudder. She was calling out: "I am finding it! I am finding the key to the cipher."

"She's only talking to waste our time," said one buccaneer. "How could a woman do in a minute what twenty men haven't done in twenty days? Shall we hoist away, Louis? Let's hear this Tranquillo screech a bit!"

"There is plenty of time for everything," said Louis d'Or. "Hold him here."

He went aft and sat on a crosspiece while the girl crouched and pointed out her discovery, only saying first,

"If I can show you something in this, Louis d'Or, is it worth anything to Ivor Kildare?"

"Is that his name?" asked the Frenchman.

"It is. And if he had had the treasure, would he have carried me away in an empty boat? Louis d'Or!—"

"Talk about the cipher of these carvings," said the Frenchman. "And if you can tell us enough, I'll see that your Kildare-Tranquillo, or whatever he is, lives until we touch the shore."

She looked desperately up at Louis d'Or, and then brushed a hand across her eyes as though she were casting from her the sudden panic of hope.

She pointed again to the inscription on the wood.

And with bent backs, out of which the muscles stood like arms and big fingers—for every man except the fine captain was naked to the waist—the buccaneers stared and listened. Only three had remained at the mast with the prisoner.

"I've heard it said that wherever there's a puzzle like this, the only way to solve it is to notice repetitions," said the girl. "If letters are spelled here, we ought to be able to make out some of them by the repetitions. But there aren't many repetitions except in the hands. Do you see? There are many hands; some of them have one finger extending, and some have two, or three, or four, or five."

"For the five vowels!" exclaimed Louis d'Or. "But still there's no sense to be made out of it. What words are meant by the mountain, the ship, the skull and crossbones?"

"I don't know. It may all be a hard thing to work out. And half of it may be used to confuse the reader. But you notice that every word begins with a capital? Suppose we use only the capitals, and the hands are the vowels—do you see?"

"There's something in that," said Louis d'Or. "What else?"

"I don't know. I'm trying to see, and in a little more time—for the sake of the kind God, Monsieur Louis d'Or—"

"For the sake of our hides!" shouted a voice. "D'you see what's blown up into the sky right over us?"

THEY LOOKED AS the long brown arm pointed. It seemed to Kildare that the thing was a bit of magic—and white magic it seemed in his eyes. For that ship which had been a blue ghost in the distance, at dawn, had grown upon the buccaneers during all of the time they searched the small boat and then examined the mind of their prisoner and listened to the explanations of the girl.

A huge galleon, it had lifted its courses above the sea, and then all its hull. The wind over its starboard quarter, leaning with the good breeze, and every sail bagful of air, it came rushing with its white bow waves running out on either side. It was near enough for the men to be marked aloft, and for the eye to follow the glimmering rounds of the muzzles of the cannon. Those rounded bows, that hull towering up fore and aft, to Kildare was swelled and loaded with a great cargo of hope.

"Up sail! Get out the sweeps!" shouted Louis d'Or. "My God, have I shipped with a crew of blind men? It's the Inquisition running at you, fools! Jump to it!"

For the great banner that shone billowing from its staff at the poop of the galleon was the flag of Spain. And Span-

ish justice for buccaneers was as neat as the way of a cat
with a mouse: not a sudden death, but a very sure one.

Kildare, jerked out of the way, was thrust aside; there was
a creaking of ropes, a rattling of the heavy handles of the
sweeps against the tholes. And then he heard the voice of
Louis d'Or again:

"Get the girl into the small boat and cast it off. She's
enough to stop them for a minute."

It was done.

"Let him come with me!" she cried. "Captain Louis
d'Or—"

The long oars ruthlessly pushed the little boat away,
heeling it over with their pressure. Then the wind put its
heavy shoulder into the sail of the periagua, the sweeps
gave it headway, they began to run, gathering speed in
impulses like the conscious efforts of a good horse, while
the small boat fell astern, paying off till its broadside was
turned to the wind.

Ines stood at the prow, waving, smiling. She would not
have him remember her with a weeping face.

Above the shouting of the buccaneers he could hear her
calling his name, a music that grew smaller than a ghost
on the wind. Her features blurred. Still he could see the
flash of her waving hand and then the brightness of her
hair turning dim until at last she was a shadow.

He had not spoken. He could not have uttered a word.
The taste of death had been in his mouth a little before, and
now sorrow was more bitter than salt in his throat.

3

A CLOSE CALL

THE SPANIARD HAD grown still higher in the sky, but now he backed his mainsail suddenly. He would, after all, pause a moment to pick up Ines Heredia from the boat. A shout of joy came ringing from the throats of the buccaneers. They were standing with mighty effort as they gave their weight to the big sweeps.

"Set Tranquillo's hands free. Let him come aft!" called Louis d'Or.

So Kildare found himself at the side of the Frenchman, who, like a good sailor, was watching the leech of his sail, not the looming enemy behind.

"If they take us, they take you with us, and all the squalling of the girl will never keep your neck out of a noose. We only have to name you Tranquillo. Then the hanging they failed to give you at Porto Bello they'll furnish you with now."

"That's all as true as a book," agreed Kildare.

"Then lend me your brains," said Louis d'Or. "If you can think of anything that will put more wind in the sail or grease the bottom of this boat for us, let me know. Because the wind is growing, Tranquillo, and that Spanish tub with all her tophamper is bound to blow up to us before long."

Kildare was looking aft. He said, still staring astern:

"They're picking up the boat now. But they've already lost nearly all their way.

"Take a slant into the wind as close as you can bring her and let every man spring on the oars. And when you're in the eye of the wind, crossing the bows of the galleon, down sail and with your sweeps carry straight on against the wind as straight a line as you can rule. The galleon can only follow by tacking—and you have a chance in three of beating her. These fellows of yours have muscles enough to use them for a long while."

"If I cross her bows, as you say," pondered Louis d'Or, "we'll come within good cannon shot."

"Aye, and of course. But Spaniards are not good at the big guns, and the small ones won't reach you."

"If a single shot caroms on the water and cracks the periagua, we're gone."

"True," said Kildare, and was silent, watching.

The darkness suddenly left the face of Louis d'Or. He shouted:

"Do you hear? You're sea-dogs now, but if the Dons catch you, you'll be dog-meat. And in this wind they'll overhaul us if we run before the breeze. We're going to cross her bows and row into the wind. That brings us under her guns. A single shot will lame us to a walk. Is there a voice against it?"

A good, deep roar came from every throat:

"Into the wind, Captain Louis! Into the wind, Louis d'Or, and chance the damned guns!"

So they turned, slowly, on account of the length of the narrow boat. Edging well into the wind, the leech of the sail began to tremble; and Kildare, as he sprang to an oar, saw the mainsail of the galleon filled again. She towered like a white mountain in the sky, and by the size of her bow wave she had almost gathered full way again.

"Now down sail, down with the mast also!" called Kildare.

"D'ye hear?" thundered Louis d'Or. "Down sail and mast! Jump to it, lads!"

They sprang to it for their lives.

By the look of them, one could tell that Louis d'Or was one who could pick and choose when he selected a crew in Tortuga or Jamaica. There was not a small man in the lot; there was not a soul of them without the brawn of a bull. A few of them ran down the sail and took down and stowed the mast, while the other kept on straining at the oars.

But there was a grim loss of way, all this while; and as the freshening wind met the periagua, lean and long as it was, it seemed to blow the boat to a stop. Anxiously, Kildare measured the diminished distance.

THE SPANIARD, COMING up on a good slant, and sailing far closer to the wind than his blunt bows would have led a sailor to expect, was bowling along closer and closer. He had come to such a near distance that the uproar of cheering on the crowded decks became like the rushing of a storm wind. And even single voices could be picked out of the tumult.

A white flag of mist appeared at his bows, blew away. There was a sound overhead like the tearing of strong canvas; and then the sea leaped up in a bright flash far beyond the side of the periagua.

A groan came out of the buccaneers, then, as though

the cannon ball had struck their life with a heavy wound. Even Kildare, who knew guns with a rare experience, was surprised by the range of that cannon, for the Spaniards as a rule favored many small guns, the English a few great ones. However, this looked like an exception that would ruin the men of Louis d'Or.

He, however, stood up with a fine courage in the stern, steering right into the eye of the wind and shouting encouragement.

"A little way uphill, and then all the rest of the way down. Pull till your backs crack. Lay out straight and stretch yourselves. Well done, Olaf! *Hai*, Peters, bend your oar, but don't break it!—Aha, my wild bulls, now that you charge all together, let's see what happens!"

Four flags of the deadly white blew now at the bows of the Spaniard; the quadruple roar of the bullets overhead joined with the brief, chattering thunder of the reports, and every man ducked his head saving Ivor Kildare and Louis d'Or.

Three balls plumped into the sea beyond the periagua. One landed so close to the stern that the wave it threw tipped the frail boat a little. It was very excellent shooting.

"There is some damned renegade English dog on board the Spaniard. Or a French dog who's thrown his soul away into the Spanish hands. No Spaniard ever shot so near a mark. Give way, my lads!" shouted Louis d'Or. "Now, Tranquillo! What do you say to my jolly fellows?"

"If you couldn't conquer a kingdom with 'em, you could rob the king, at least," answered Kildare.

And there was breath enough left in two or three throats to laugh a little.

The only black man of the lot, a creature who looked like an ape, with a forward thrusting head on a vast neck that was overgrown with hair almost to the shoulders, now pitched his head to the side and burst into a rousing song, with a wail and a yell to it that maintained a strong rhythm. Kildare could not understand the obscurely pronounced words, but he saw that a new life came into the crew. They bent to their oars with a longer sweep.

They jumped to that rhythm until the periagua leaped more and more quickly ahead.

And now they had come, certainly, to the critical moment. Those great bow guns of the galleon must be close to perfect range, and the periagua, if it remained unscathed for a few more minutes, was certain to draw away to safety.

Once more the smoke puffed from the bows. Something rushed like a viewless devil past the ear of Kildare. A wind pulled like invisible hands at his flesh. And right alongside a shot plumped into the water and hurled a column of sea into the air and on board them, blown by the wind. Two other shots had fallen short as Louis d'Or shouted:

"Overboard with him! The best part of him is left, but we can't use it!"

Kildare turned and saw a headless body lifted and flung into the water.

IT DID NOT sink at once, but lay in the midst of a spreading stain of red. Then a curving spin rose above the surface, furrowed the water.

He could see the long, pale belly of the shark—and the dead body disappeared.

Even Louis d'Or was silenced by a thought for a moment after this. From the Spanish ship a great voice of disappointment came howling across the water as though pouring from a single throat.

Immediately another four-gun volley was fired, but all of these shots fell well astern.

It was plain then that the Spaniard, in his eagerness, had made a great mistake in sailing. He had brought his ship too near to the wind, and now the fore-topsail was taken aback, spatting the mast with a noise as loud as a handclap close to the ears. The galleon shuddered visible and then paid off. It was a vital distance that had been lost.

"Easier now, my lads!" called Louis d'Or. "Easier, easier! We've sailed through the mouth of the tiger and only been scratched by one of his teeth. But if this damned wind keeps freshening we'll have the Spaniard up with us again. Steady, and a long stroke should tell the story for us."

Half the strain was taken from the heaving bodies of the oarsmen, but still the sweeps worked with what seemed hardly less power than before.

The Spaniard, if he had been put out of cannon range for the moment, was not entirely disheartened. He began tacking into the wind, sailing on courses that swept him back and forth. As a heron beats up into the sky with the strokes of his hollow wings cupping the air while the falcon swims swiftly around the horizon and so mounts, in the same manner the long boat was urged by the oars against a windy river of the sea while the ranging galleon swung back and forth and at every tack came closer to its target; for the rowers were beginning to feel exhaustion.

Their heads dropped to this side or to that and there remained. Their mouths pulled at the corners so that they seemed to be grinning. The cords of their necks thrust out. Their bodies were all in a tremble.

Louis d'Or pulled his long rapier twice half out of the scabbard as he looked at the galleon over his shoulder. Then he stared at Kildare and asked:

"Well, you had one bit of good advice in your head; have you any other?"

"Yes," said Kildare. "To rest on our oars and breathe ourselves, then run back at them and fight."

He had hardly said this when the wind blew a good, hearty gust that tipped every wave with white; then the breeze died down suddenly, the waves fell into a welter of unquietness, merely, and when they looked back they saw the sails of the galleon hanging loosely down like the cheeks of an old man.

The heads of the rowers dropped forward; slowly they oared away, and every stroke took them that exact distance from the galleon until the hull of it dropped into the sea again, and then the courses sank into the blue, and the blue itself ran up, like a dye soaked from the sea, until all the upper sails were stained also.

4

A CIPHER REVEALED

THEY LAY—LITERALLY—ON THEIR oars, with their heads fallen forward and tipped up and down as the waves swayed irregularly the long blades of the sweeps. They could thank the lightness of the cedar boat for letting them escape from the wind and the Spaniard by force of their muscles only.

Louis d'Or said, "Brothers of the coast!" and every head was jerked up suddenly.

"Here," said Louis d'Or, who remained standing in the stern as he had all through the crisis of the chase, looking bigger and more master of himself and the crew than ever before, "here is this Tranquillo the Second, who chased the first Tranquillo and killed him in a fair fight. With enough brains in his head to help us away from the Spaniard, he is still among us. But the treasure of Tranquillo is not with us. Now, brothers, give me your voices. What shall we do with him?"

The shortest man of the crew was the one who answered first. He was an Irishman, the shortest of all the buccaneers, but much the broadest. He had blue eyes and a skin that never would be sun-blackened but burned into freckles that looked like dark blisters. The tip of his nose turned up and was cooked constantly red and raw by the sun. He spent a good deal of his time touching the raw tip with a tentative forefinger, and then looking at his finger to see if it had brought any of the singed skin away.

His name was Padraic, so he was called Pat. He spoke up in a voice curiously high and whining, like a dog in a cold night whining outside the door of a house:

"I would like to see Tranquillo's sword, first of all. We can talk after we've seen his sword."

"Why do you want to see his sword?" asked Louis d'Or.

"Well," said Pat, "I knew a Portuguese that had been in Kingston, and the Portuguese knew a Finn that had sailed with Tranquillo the First and Tranquillo the Second. He said that this English-Italian had a sword no bigger than a needle, but he had a way with it of making a dazzle in the eyes of a man, and then stabbing him through the brain or heart.

"You would have said that a wasp had stung the man, or a hornet. Three drops of blood, and the man was dead. He said—the Finn did—that a good ax, or a machete, or a broadsword with an armored man swinging it, or even a rapier in the hands of a dancing, prancing fencing man like Louis d'Or was no damned good against that needle in the hands of Tranquillo the Second. That's why I want to see the sword."

Louis d'Or looked curiously at Kildare.

"Draw your sword," he said.

Kildare drew it out of the sheath and made a fencer's salute to the three points of the compass. Then he held the sword straight up before him. It was a mere shred, a spindling shard of steel. It was hard to imagine it drawn out to its proper length, and terminating with a needle-like point.

"I'd as soon fight with a moonbeam in my fist!" said the Irishman, staring. "Man, how did you come to fight by such a bit of a thing as that even before it was broken short?"

Kildare said, "I was once in a fight, my arm aching from the weight of a rapier, and a strong parry shivered the rapier, and left not very much more than half its length and a mere splinter of the steel. But just when I told myself that I was to die, I found that the weight was gone from my arm, my feet were light—and though the sword was gone, there was always the point, the point, the point!"

He raised his voice, laughed, and shot the little blade back into its meager scabbard.

"Now in a good, hard fight," said the Irishman, "when you stand close, and it's sweating and straining, and no room to dance—like a fight on shipboard, we'll say—you mean that that little thing, that needle, is anything against the good whanging weight of a machete that had been ground sharp?"

"Well, my friend," said Kildare, "did you ever fight with a wasp that is always ready to sting?"

THERE HAD BEEN some murmuring up and down the long periagua during this talk. Now the talk all died away. They remembered that ray of bright steel in the hand of Kildare, and wondered. Perhaps the sting of that wasp would mean the death.

"Talkin' in this way," said the Irishman, "I say, give Tranquillo the riddle to read. If he reads it by dark, let him be one of us. If he can't read it, let him do more good to the belly of a shark than he's doing to any of us!"

The thought seemed good to the rest. With one shout they agreed.

That was how the thing was set. Kildare sat down by the puzzle and pondered over it.

He began where the girl had left off and took her suggestions as though they were inspired. For he had a respect for mind. He himself, without any weight of hand or bigness of body, had managed to hold his own among fighting men. Quick hands and feet had done part of it. Quick wits had done far more.

A man can never be swifter than his brain. And the girl might have done what the gravest man in the world with a library of books would never accomplish.

Kildare, through the heat of the middle day neither ate or drank. He felt neither thirst nor hunger, for his mind drifted strangely between the thought of Ines Heredia and the sense that his own life might end when the sun went down.

He kept going back to the beginning, on her presumption. If the hands were vowels, how would one begin, supposing that only the first letters of the words counted?

"Saqsf—" "Seqsf—" "Soqsf—" It made no difference what vowel he put in the place of the hand, using the first letters of the words, he arrived at no sense.

"Now," said a voice finally, after an age of time, "the sun is getting into the west, Tranquillo." That was Louis d'Or speaking.

There were so many "t's" in the last words that they stuck in the mind of Kildare. Instead of the "S" of "Safe," he read "T."

T-a-q-s-f that made no sense, either.

But it seemed nearer to something.

Then it came to him that the first letters, the consonants,

might not represent their own positions in the alphabet. The letter before "S" was "R." So, substituting in the case of each initial consonant the letter that went before it, he came to "R-A-P-R," which was an unlikely beginning, even if he used any other vowel in the place of the "A."

Instead of taking the letter before, he would try the vowel after.

This made: "T-A-R-T—"

THE BRAIN AND heart of Kildare leaped. That westering sun was already golden in the west. Soon it would be red, and then it would drop like a stone and leave the world to the quick rush of the tropic darkness, like, a flight of black wings. He had to hurry. But this was like the beginning of a word. "Tart—" Then came another hand. Call it "A" again. "T-A-R-T-A-G-A—"

As he spelled out the word, "Tartaga," it seemed to him perfect nonsense, and then into his mind jumped a very similar sound: "Tortuga," that island whose humped back looked like a great turtle. Tortuga—that must be right, and he had reached suddenly to the key of the riddle! But there must be more to come. A hand with four fingers means "O," with five fingers, "U," with one finger, "A." Why then, since the vowels were ordered a, e, i, o, u, the fingers were apportioned in number to the place of the vowel in the alphabet.

This was light indeed. Of the sign of the sailing ship he could make nothing. He disregarded it and rushed on to the initial letters and the hands again. So he spelled out at once: "t-h-r-e-e."

He jumped the compass sign and hurried on still farther. The next made "S-t-e-p-s—"

He could have shouted aloud.

"Tortuga—three—steps—" this was sense and there were words, no matter how obscure their meaning.

He went on, always disregarding designs, no matter how complicated.

And the message that he deciphered now read: "Tortuga—three—steps—from—the—black—rock—to—Dutch—John."

The signs, therefore, were nothing. Nothing but terminals to signify the end of a word and betray the searcher into a vain inquiry into some pictorial meaning.

On Tortuga there was something three steps away from the black rock towards the step of Dutch John. That was the meaning.

What was the thing? Why, it was merely the place where that great treasure of jewels was located, of course!

The sun slid down like a man ducking his head beneath a bank.

"I have it," said Kildare, looking up.

There was an ache in the back of his neck, and he rubbed himself there.

It seemed to him that the eyes of Louis d'Or were green with light, like emeralds.

"What have you?" asked the captain.

"Is there one of you that knows Dutch John?" asked Kildare.

"Dutch John that died of the fever on Tortuga?" asked one of the men. "I never knew him. But I've been drunk with him a few times."

"Do you know where he was buried? Near black rocks?"

"I don't know a thing about rocks, but I helped dig the

grave where we laid him. It was a queer thing that he was
so fat his body begun to stink less than a day after he died."

"There is a black rock near his grave," said Kildare. "This
is what the writing of Tranquillo says: 'Tortuga, three steps
from the black rock to Dutch John.' And that's where we'll
find the treasure buried."

They were tired men, but they began a great yelling. The
sun dipped down, suddenly, and the darkness ran without
a star over the sea.

Three days later they had beached the periagua on a
white lee shore when at the suggestion of Louis d'Or, the
blacksmith's anvil was set up and he was put to work forg-
ing a new blade for the sword of Kildare; and since he used
a bit of fine Toledo steel and was a high master in the art of
tempering subtle, strong steel, his work was a masterpiece.

5

SUDDEN MUTINY

THEY REACHED TORTUGA, humped out of the water like the back of a turtle. Closer in, they entered the narrow waters between that little island and Hispaniola, and here the periagua was run into a cove and beached. Luis was left to guard the boat. It was still half a mile down the beach to the reported grave of Dutch John, and the men marched rapidly. The water rolled and creamed on their right. On the left rose the big, dark cedars and a crowded growth of clammy cherry, dogwood, fustic, lignum-vitæ, logwood, gru-gru palms, and always masses of ferns at every interval.

"Why should Dutch John be buried so far from the anchorage?" demanded Louis d'Or.

"Because," said a buccaneer, "the fever he had was the catching kind. We threw dice to see what men would go bury him at a distance, and I was one of the unlucky ones. However, the fever never came out on me.—There," he added, "is the place—somewhere in there. Aye, and here it is!"

He ran forward suddenly and stopped at a point where half a dozen heavy stones were piled one above the other to make a squat little pyramid. "This is the place!" he declared, still pointing down.

And all about him the buccaneers halted, breathless, staring about them for a sign of the black rock which now meant so much. A cloud of mosquitoes poured like a lazy smoke out of the woods and began to settle for blood but not a hand rose to brush them away.

Then the Irishman ran and beat aside a tall growth of ferns, trampling them down. Behind them, glistening with the jungle sweat like the head of a living beast, appeared a black rock that jutted two feet or more above the ground. A low, groaning sound of relief came from the men.

Pat, turning, made three long strides from the rock towards the gravestones of Dutch John. He halted, stamping his feet into the ground.

"Here!" he said. "This would be the place!"

They began to dig, some with their hands, and some with a pair of adzes which made very good hoes, though the carpenter cursed when he saw the delicate edge of the steel being brought down on rocks.

All in a moment a hole was yawning. Suddenly a hand lifted something between thumb and forefinger. It shone in the sun with a yellow glitter.

"Gold! Gold!" shouted the discoverer. "The treasure is here! We have found it!"

"It is here, sure enough!" said a tall German called Johann. "Then, rally to me, my mates!—Keep the captain's third for ourselves! Down with that damned whip-using, murdering Louis d'Or! At them, masters!"

The crowd formed into two quick swirls, Louis d'Or and a narrow cluster of men in the center, with the negro, the Irishman, and three others, and about them more than twice that number. Some thirteen or fourteen to six made up the tale of the odds. Most were armed with machetes, in the play of which they were almost as scientific as any gentleman dancing with his rapier. The German, Johann, carried an axe on the end of a long handle. One fellow was content with his adze.

There was an instant death. One of the mutineers struck his heavy machete down through the left shoulder of the negro as deep as the lungs. The black man should have fallen in an agony. Instead, he fought as a tiger fights, even after a bullet has touched its heart. The other, trying to jerk his weapon free from the flesh, pulled the negro towards him. The black stumbled to his knees, coughing blood.

The machete was knocked out of his hand by the fall, but he pulled a long, curved knife out of his belt and stabbed upwards into the belly of his murderer. Still on his knees, he struck right and left.

A second mutineer went down; a third was deeply wounded in the leg.

The fight was now regular. There were no firearms. They had been left in the boat by the command of the captain. Therefore the battle was hand to hand; Louis d'Or with his long rapier standing like a tower in the war, and four others working in a circle around his back. A dozen mutineers were striving to break through that living guard.

AS FOR KILDARE, the beach was open and his way was clear. If he had been half a prisoner even after solving the riddle of Tranquillo's message, he was now able to seize on his freedom at once.

In fact, he turned and made a step or two. But the moment that his back was turned, it seemed to him that the clash of the steel and the howling of the fighters redoubled; it blew like a trumpet in his ears, and in a moment he had whirled and drawn that slender sword of his, shouting: "Louis d'Or! Louis d'Or!"

A pair of the mutineers immediately in front of him jumped about to face that attack from the rear. They struck with their machetes at the same time, full at his head. He stepped just outside the sweep of the weapons, as a feather is knocked back by the wind of a handstroke. For a subtle instant their hands were down and in that instant he had sprung in. His sword flashed. He was out again. The point of his blade no longer was brilliant as a ray of sunlight. Some small drops ran from it and one of the mutineers dropped his machete, grasped his throat with both hands, and began to gasp and choke.

"*Hai,* Juan—are you down?" cried his companion. And then: "Here's for you, Tranquillo!—I'll make you tranquil!—I'll give you a long sleep!—Brother Juan, watch me pay your score before you die."

He was letting drive a maze of strokes at Kildare as he shouted, charging in wildly, for the fallen man was his sworn companion after that habit of the buccaneers of choosing a brother who would guard a man's back in a time of danger.

Kildare danced back two steps. The delicate blade of his rapier engaged the furious machete with a touch soft as silk, but which nevertheless turned the mighty strikes awry. Then the sword darted in and out. The eye could hardly tell whether or not it had touched the flesh, but the buccaneer fell dead on his face.

That was how a gap was made in the circle of the assailants, as Kildare sprang in to the side of Louis d'Or. The

Frenchman had been wounded by a grazing edge high on his head; the blood reddened half his face and dripped rapidly down over his finery, but he kept laughing like a happy devil as he fought.

He had lost another man; still another was mortally wounded and fought with his body leaning over, his hand clasped to his gashed side. It was murder, not battle. Eight mutineers against five of the captain's side; and one of the five a dying man. And yet there was still a chance that resided in the educated hands of Kildare and Louis d'Or.

The captain shouted: "Brave Tranquillo!—Heart of my heart! By God, I love you, and we'll die together laughing. Do you hear, Caspar?"

"I hear," sighed the wounded man.

"You are dead anyway. Be a useful man and run in, let them kill you ten times more, but cut the throat of Johann for us."

Gaspar, without a word of response, straightened and uttered a wild yell. The blood burst in a torrent from his wounded side yet he rushed straight at Johann. The long axe struck him down, horribly hurt. He leaped up again and clove the skull of big Johann like a block of soft wood with a hatchet.

KILDARE SAW THAT from the corner of his eye. He had watched two of the mutineers fall back a step, speak to one another, and now they bore straight in on him with a rush. He knew the meaning of that. One of them might die, but the other was almost sure to flesh his machete in the throat or the body of Kildare; and men did not survive such strokes as the brush knives were capable of giving. They were two more sworn brothers.

One of them was a mere boy of twenty, big as he was. He had fair hair so light that it blew about his head and face as he ran in, shouting. The other either was prematurely bald in front or had shaved himself to look like a Mongol, and wore his remaining hair in two dangling pigtails down his back. He bounded high in the air as he reached at Kildare; the second lad ran in low.

Fencing would not save Kildare then. He flung his narrow-bladed sword like a dart right into the body of the older buccaneer. A side-step snaked him away from the machete of the second. He caught the man by the sword wrist.

It was like laying hold of a piece of wood, grained and knotted with hard tendons. Instantly the youngster had him by the throat and jerked his machete free. It had done work before, and the bright steel of it was filmed over with a shining skin of purple. Body to body, there was no room for Kildare to work but he had pulled from his belt a poniard that matched his rapier—a dripping icicle of steel, a veritable needle. With that he stabbed the mutineer twice under the arm.

Something thudded heavily against his head. It was the machete fallen from a dead hand. The loose, heavy body poured down through the arms of Kildare and lay at his feet. He leaped over it. He of the pigtails lay on his face with a glittering span or so of the sword projecting from the center of his back. Kildare jerked him up by the braided hair and whipped out the weapon. The hilt was slippery with blood, but the blade was all intact.

He turned, and saw that the battle was ended.

The Irishman, covered with blood and brains, had struck

the last resisting mutineer through the head and was stepping back, now, panting heavily. And tall Louis d' Or was spotted red from head to foot.

These and Kildare was only three who remained standing out of twenty-one chosen men who had been alive and well ten minutes before.

The whole place was sopping red. The stones of the beach were slippery with blood that was still welling.

Of the captain's group there were three dead; the captain himself hurt in a trifling manner in the head; the Irishman with only a shallow gash on his left arm; and Kildare untouched.

Of the mutineers in that famous and murderous battle, eight men were killed outright, three died of their wounds at once and two were deliberately butchered under the eyes of Kildare by the captain, who ran the long blade of his rapier calmly through their bodies. One of the entire fourteen remained. He was that same fellow who had been hurt in the leg by the negro, and he had received other wounds before he staggered back helplessly and fell at the foot of a tree with blood running out of him fast. But he had worn a small brandy flask at his belt and this was now in his hand.

He lifted it and called out: "To your health, my captain! Dig up the treasure and let me see the shine of the jewels of Tranquillo before I go to sleep."

The captain stalked towards the man with his red sword in his hand but Kildare caught his arm and drew him back.

"The man's dying," he said.

"I've killed two on their feet and two on the ground," said the captain, "and that would make five for my tale."

"Let him be," said Kildare.

"I give him to you—the dog!" said the captain. "Look, Tranquillo! How God favors me! He wipes out the worthless vermin with whom I should have had to share the treasure we are about to uncover, but more than that, He gives me on the same day a blood-brother worth more than a passport into heaven. Give me your hand!—Here, Pat— your hand also. Here are we three with the manifest sign of God on us and a red world under our feet. Shall we be true to one another?"

THEY STOOD IN a closed circle with blood dripping from the slippery hands which were clenched together.

"Would I be fool enough to have another man near me, after this day's work? Captain, you've done with four of them, but two were on the ground. And this dancing man, this Tranquillo—his ugly mug looks beautiful to me with the blood on it! He killed four fighting men with the fight still in them. My eyes have seen it! Are we brothers, Tranquillo?"

"We are," said Kildare, looking deep into the eyes of the Irishman.

"And I am one!" exclaimed Louis d'Or. He recited: "My hand is your hand—"

As he paused the other two repeated the familiar oath: "My hand is your hand—"

Then all three went on together:

"… my eye is your eye, my blood is your blood. Amen!"

That oath had sealed many a hard-fighting pair of buccaneers to a single fortune; but it never before had linked three together.

6

PANAMA LURE

WITH THE BLOOD still unwashed from them, they picked up the adzes and began to dig furiously at the hole which already had been opened.

The dying mutineer began to sing new words to an old tune, keeping the time with the sway of his brandy flask.

> *Louis d'Or, Louis d'Or,*
> *We were twenty men and more,*
> *Louis d'Or.*
> *And we sailed and we sailed*
> *Till the Dew of Heaven jailed,*
> *Louis d'Or.*
> *Louis d'Or, Louis d'Or,*
> *We have changed the gold for gore,*
> *Louis d'Or.*
> *Light the candle, ring the bell,*
> *For we'll sing our song in hell,*
> *Louis d'Or.*

Here the adze in the hand of the Irishman rang on metal. They shouted, and instantly had out of the pebbles a box of rusted iron. A stroke with an adze sprung it open.

For a moment, so strong and fierce was the expectation, it seemed to Kildare that the box was brimmed with red and green and white lights of priceless gems. And then his brain clearing, he saw that there was only a folded piece of paper.

"This?" shouted the captain, lifting the paper. "Is this what we find? Look, Tranquillo! Look, Pat! There are eighteen men that have died for the sake of sharing—a damned rag of paper!"

He spread out the sheet, and the eyes of Kildare pondered a design far stranger than that which dead Tranquillo had carved on the side of his periagua but patently from the same brain.

The Irishman was tying up his bleeding arm and saying, philosophically, "It's only a bit of paper chase, lads. That damned ghost of Tranquillo will run us around and around the world before we're through with him."

Here the buccaneer beneath the tree burst into a great, mocking laughter that snapped short. He rolled over on his face and began to beat the pebbles with his hands and feet like a child on the floor, helpless with mirth. Then, as though a hand had touched him, he lay suddenly still.

"It has cost us," said Louis d'Or, "eighteen lives and other troubles to find—a piece of paper. Tranquillo, you've had fortune with you when you looked at the design the fool cut on the side of the periagua. Can you do anything with this?"

Kildare sat down on the beach, cross-legged, and peered at the document. The others stared over his shoulders. The blood was drying on his body, pulling at the skin as it turned hard. The mosquitoes, singing their small song through the wash of the sea waters, gathered unnoticed about the three.

"A cat, a rat, a dog, a mule, a bee, an owl, a cat again," said Kildare. "Then a bow and arrow, a coronet and a crown, a cannon, a twig of flowers, a sword scratched out, a flower again. What the devil is there to say about that?"

"Repetitions, said the girl," remarked Louis d'Or. "Repetitions are the things to look for in the solving of a cipher.—Ah, there's a brain in that girl, Tranquillo. I don't wonder that you preferred her with empty hands to any of the damned mincing fools, that most men meet. Beauty kills brains, as a rule. But God made her face the foreword, the true title page of the whole book of her. She would be worth half the treasure if she were here to work out this riddle for us."

"She minded me," said the Irishman, Padraic, "of a girl I left behind me in the old country—except that Tranquillo's lady has bright hair and mine had black, and Tranquillo's is short and mine is tally and Tranquillo's is slender and mine would fill a door—"

"Then how did she remind you of your girl in Ireland?" asked the captain.

"How can I tell?" exclaimed Padraic. "But all at once I thought of her. Because there's woman in them both, I suppose."

Kildare said, "Suppose you look at it in another way. There are living things, flowers, weapons, numbers. Four kinds. For what? For vowels? And why not? All the five vowels may not be used. But no, there are signs over letters, and perhaps they stand for the fourth vowel."

"What are the words that are written down?" asked Louis d'Or.

"Ma — no — me — you — rej — he — ya — wake — naya — joy," read Kildare. "That's hard to make sense of, eh?"

"Aye, but most of the things must have meanings," said the captain. "That is, if he wrote down a sentence of any length. Well, as your lady pointed out—five sorts of things would mean the five vowels, eh? Then try the consonants the way you did before, and use only the first ones."

Kildare shook his head. He could feel the struggle ahead of him increasing every moment.

"Let me think!" he begged. "I'll sit here till I've found the answer."

Dimly he could hear the captain and the Irishman conversing and agreeing that it would be a hopeless task to bury so many dead men. They could be left to birds and flies and beasts. So the two collected, calmly, the weapons and the money belts of the dead and went back with heavy arm-loads towards the boat.

Finally, after much working, the deciphered message read, "Panama behind peacocks tail San Francisco."

He stood up, stretched the numbness out of his legs, and walked past the dead men, past the gloomy cedars, to the periagua, where Louis d'Or and the Irishman had succeeded in launching the long boat on a rising tide. Over the side he sprang and laid his solution before them.

"Panama behind peacocks tail San Francisco. What does that mean? Which of you has been in Panama?"

"I," said Louis d'Or.

"What could a peacock in Panama mean?"

"You have the message wrong," said the Irishman. "What would the meaning be in such a thing?"

Kildare looked down at his encrusted hands and began to wash them in the sea water.

"Try again," he said. "What does San Francisco have to do with Panama?"

"THERE'S A CHURCH of San Francisco in Panama," said Louis d'Or. "A Franciscan church, at any rate. Would that answer?"

"Ah," said Kildare. "Of course it answers. In Panama in the Church Of St. Francis—there's the start. Well, in the Church of St. Francis in Panama there is a peacock, believe it if you can. And behind the tail of the peacock is the treasure of Tranquillo."

"In the church?" shouted the Irishman. "Why would the fool hide it in a church?"

"Where would a man be less likely to look for treasure than in one of the nooks and crannies of a church?" asked Louis d'Or. "The thing's done, my lads! Somewhere in the church of San Francisco in Panama. Somewhere we find a peacock—done in stone, most likely. And behind the peacock's tail is the treasure of that poor Tranquillo! *Hai*, Tranquillo the Second—why would the fool write down such things? He could remember his secret, couldn't he?"

"Why," said Kildare, "the life of a buccaneer is not much surer than a candle in a blowing wind. And it may be that Tranquillo had a partner in the adventure and that they agreed between them to leave some record of what they had done and where they had lodged the treasure."

"Aye," said Louis d'Or, "and suppose also that Tranquillo with his lot was a hunted man through the streets of Panama—as any but a Spaniard is apt to be chased—he might very well have slipped into the bigness of the church to hide himself."

"And now?" said the Irishman. "Why should we rub our hands and warm ourselves as if we had a fire on a cold night? It's a long cry from here to Panama—and damned hard for a man to get into the town if he has an English look about him."

"The treasure is not ours, but it shall be," answered Louis d'Or. "Shall we go to the anchorage and try to exchange this periagua for a smaller canoa, perhaps?"

"No," said Kildare, "but we can pick up a few extra hands and make the voyage in this boat. She's as quick as a fish in the water. And she'll ride lighter with a smaller crew.— What are you thinking of, Louis d'Or?"

"Of Johann, and how he went down. The dog! I fed him when he was starving."

"He's a fire-eater," said the Irishman, "and where he is now, he'll never starve again."

After that, no one of them ever spoke again of the dead men on the beach.

7

TOWARD PORTO BELLO

WHEN THEY WENT down the beach, well weighted down by the load of weapons which they were carrying, they were amazed to find that the periagua was gone, and Luis, of course, with it. The Irishman and Louis d'Or began to curse the Mosquito, but Kildare told them, simply:

"If he's gone, it's because he was taken. What's been happening behind this headland we can't tell. Men may have come coasting toward the town and picked up the periagua on the way. It had the look that would take the eye of any Brother of the Coast."

They cached the weapons they did not need and went on up the beach rapidly until, rounding a little peninsula, they came in view of the town of Tortuga, which had been whittled out of the jungle by the labor of buccaneers and their slaves and apprentices.

Kildare, as he saw the place, remembered how, on a day, he had fought the real Tranquillo for the right to use that name; and he gripped his fists so hard that the newly healed wounds in the hollow of his left hand began to burn and ache.

It was as quiet a looking place as one could wish to see. It had not streets, really, but green strips of ground that wandered among the houses, and the houses themselves were little huts carelessly built, for the most part, except where some merchant had put up an ambitious warehouse near the water's edge. Under the trees hammocks were hung; a few wisps of smoke floated softly away over the roofs; an odor of cookery clung in the air. It was the sort of a place that made men relax body and mind.

And yet the work was going forward. Through the palms that shaded the huts here and there Kildare could see the glimpses of the rolling land, and the swaying figures which flashed hoes up and down monotonously, cultivating the acres of maize or of tobacco.

On the beach, newly dragged up from the sea, lay the periagua.

"You see," said Kildare, "that there were a good many hands at work on this business. If Luis had stolen the periagua, he never could have drawn it up onto the shore."

"Shall we take the boat and leave?" asked the Irishman. "Or shall we try to find the thieves and fight 'em?"

He asked with a perfect indifference as to the answer.

"Find them, and fight 'em if we have to," said the Frenchman.

They looked into the periagua and saw that its stock of muskets, ammunition, food, and all the essential supplies of a voyage were still intact. Only Luis was gone.

So the three advanced into Tortuga. They were guided by a growing uproar of voices, loud laughter, shouts; they saw a gathered crowd of such tatterdemalions as it would have been hard to find again in any part of the world.

Some of them were in the bloodstained cotton shirts and drawers of the true buccaneers, recently returned from curing beef and pork in the forests of Hispaniola; others had bought new clothes from the merchants who traded at Tortuga, and every wild color, from crimson to staring yellow was on the backs of the dandies of the Coast.

From a distance, through a gap in the crowd, the three could see what was going forward.

AN INDIAN WAS tied to a pole by a rope that bound one wrist. The other hand and his legs were free, and he had in his hand a short stick. Ten paces from him a stalwart buccaneer was bending a bow, drawing the arrows to the head and shooting them with a practiced hand straight at the Indian.

The fellow helped himself by twisting and dodging in a marvelous manner, but with his stick he struck aside every arrow as it leaped at him.

"That's a Mosquito Indian," said Louis d'Or.

"It's my man!" shouted Kildare, and came up on the run, his friends at his shoulder.

The man with the bow had stopped, wiped his forehead, damned the heat, and called for brandy from his valet—because every self-respecting buccaneer, when he was ashore or hunting pork and beef in the woods of Hispaniola, kept a body servant who was kicked and beaten through a long novitiate until he was hardened to a sufficient brutality and then became a full-fledged master buccaneer. The archer tossed off a dram of French brandy and announced:

"When I was a lad, we used to amuse ourselves shooting at pigeons tied to a string, and if I can't hit a full-sized Indian may I be damned to hell and back. Now for you!"

He took a whole step nearer and began to draw his arrow

to the head. The buccaneers shouted in anticipation and leaned forward to watch. Some of them were so newly come from hunting that they had not yet become properly drunk.

They looked like barbarians who had just plundered a civilized town and dressed themselves in the booty. This was the moment when Kildare came up on the run, shouting out that he would put a pistol bullet through the buccaneer if another arrow were fired at Luis.

The Mosquito, crouched in an agony of suspense, tense to make the next parry of the flying shaft, straightened a little.

"Hold your tongue," said the archer. "Are you one of the fools that loves Indians?"

"I don't love them, but I hate to waste them," said Kildare. "And every man here knows that a Mosquito with his spear and irons can keep a hundred head of men in fish on a decent voyage."

"Keep your talk to yourself," said the buccaneer.

"I'd rather split your tongue than hold my own," said Kildare.

The whole crowd started. "Do you hear him, Pierre?" shouted one.

Pierre, wheeling about more slowly, dropped his bow and arrow to the ground.

"Here, boy," he said to his valet, "reach me my sword."

A long, heavy cutlass was instantly put into his grasp.

"Now stand out if you dare and tell me what you are and who you are that comes between a man and his judgment on his own slave!" exclaimed Pierre.

"LET ME TAKE this fight," said the Irishman at the ear of Kildare.

"Let it be my quarrel!" murmured Louis d'Or on the opposite side.

Kildare stepped out into the open circle.

"I am Captain Tranquillo," said Kildare.

Pierre laughed.

"Then I'm Cæsar and Hannibal all in one," he said. "Why, you lying fool, Tranquillo would make two of you! He could hold enough brandy to drown you!"

"Wait!" called out a buccaneer. "This is the Englishman who chose to call himself Tranquillo and fought here with the other Tranquillo for the right to the name, and beat him!"

"Then the true Tranquillo was drunk," said Pierre. "Step up to me, liar!"

He made two or three cuts in the air with his cutlass as he spoke, and Kildare unsheathed that delicate sword of his which had drunk so much blood already this day. The sight of it had a wonderful effect on Pierre. He was a man all jowls and no brain, and a bush of whiskers made his head seem to grow directly out of his shoulders. When he saw the narrow sword in the hand of Kildare, he grunted like a pig.

"Are you ready?" he shouted. "Is that damned needle what you hope to fight with? Come to me, Tranquillo, and I'll lay you tranquil for the rest of your life with one stroke."

"You're drunk," said Kildare. "But tell me first what claim you have on this friend of mine, this Luis?"

"He's a Mosquito Indian, isn't he?" demanded Pierre.

"He is that. And what of it?"

"This of it! Was not my own Brother of the Coast murdered last year?"

"I know nothing about that," said Kildare.

"I tell you now. He was murdered. And it was a cursed Mosquito Indian that waited behind a bush and speared him through the throat just as he was taking a drink of brandy in the light of the burning hut."

"Your friend had burned down the Indian's hut?" asked Kildare.

"Yes. Because it was a wet night and we needed heat to dry our clothes.—I say that a Mosquito Indian murdered him, and I swore that I would kill the next Mosquito that I ever met.—Is that justice?"

THERE WAS A bawling shout from all the true democrats who stood around the place. "Justice! This is a judgment!"

"Very well," said Kildare, "if this is justice, let me fight for my share of it. Are you ready?"

"Ready—and not waiting!" shouted the buccaneer, and charged like a bull.

Kildare, without bothering to parry the tremendous, sweeping blow of the cutlass, side-stepped it and touched the buccaneer just between the eyes; a little trickle of blood was running down the face of the big fellow as he turned, roaring.

"That touch ought to sober you," said Kildare. "Guard yourself!"

The buccaneer, in fact, now came in more cautiously and delivered a sudden attack with great skill and judgment. The blow slithered off the supple blade of Kildare like bright drops of water.

A great shouting began to go up. "A master! A master of the sword! Pierre, you are up against witchcraft!"

Pierre suddenly drew back, uttered a cry of fury, and then flung himself in for a final effort. The rapier of Kildare leaped in and out. Pierre, ending his charge, dropped his cutlass and grasped his sword arm above the wrist. Blood forced its way through his fingers.

"Have I paid the price for Luis?" asked Kildare.

There was another universal shouting.

"Teach me one of your damned dancing tricks," said the defeated buccaneer, "and I'd give up the slaughter of a hundred Mosquitoes. Take the Indian, if you want him, and may he cut your throat for you before you're a day older."

"I take also," said Kildare, "the periagua that you and your friends carried off, and Luis along with it."

"Take what you please," said Pierre, "and be damned while you take it!"

He turned on his heel and strode away; a moment later Luis was free. But he showed not the slightest sign of rejoicing; he merely fixed on Kildare a long, bright, considering look, as though a great thought had just entered his mind.

It was a temptation for them to remain in Tortuga and relax with the good French brandy and enjoy the lazy life; but after they had bought a few supplies, on the same day of their coming they left the island, their crew rounded out by François, a strong, husky mulatto they had bought.

It was after they had left that the report came in about the dead men on the beach, and that was the origin of the story which presently traveled as far as the winds blow all over the Caribbean Sea and across the mainland.

The legend told how three men had fought eighteen and left the eighteen dead, while only two of the three were so much as scratched.

It never occurred to a single man that among the dead might lie some of those who had fought with the minority. **THEY HAD LITTLE** wind, but enough to give them steerageway day after day, and they used the lazy hours of leisure to elaborate their plans. As for Kildare, he wished merely to be taken to Porto Bello, where, he was sure, Ines Heredia had been carried before him. If she were gone, he first would cross the Isthmus with his two companions and make the wild attempt to find the treasure of Tranquillo. And after that they would help him, as in honor bound, to recover his lady. This compact they made in detail.

The mulatto and the Indian, after they reached the western coast, would be left to guard the periagua after it had been beached and hidden away in some obscure place.

They might not be able to trust François farther than they could see him, but the Mosquito Indian was a rock of trust.

Luis, couched in the bows with his pronged spear ready, kept them in more fresh fish than they could eat. He helped to kill time for them, also, by telling them—in the starlight, which was the only time when he would talk—stories about the life of his people.

The last day came, with a good wind at last bowling them forward, and the periagua leaping along like a flying fish, when the Mosquito Indian cried out that he could see the shore.

Actually, the others strained their eyes for another fifteen minutes before they could make out the loom of the land, so wonderfully acute were the eyes of the Indian.

At last they saw opening the mouth of the fine bay of Porto Bello, and the hills that ringed the city around with a fine mist creeping upward, like a smoke from the city.

Here their next adventure was to take place. They became grim and silent as they stared toward the land.

8

IN PORTO BELLO

THE SUN WENT down. In the instant darkness which followed, they entered the bay, sliding close to the "Iron Castle" on the western point. Henry Morgan had ruined the fort when he gnawed Porto Bello to the marrow of its bones not long before, and burned the town behind him. But the Spaniards simply moved in hordes of slaves and rebuilt the place.

They had to have a western port for the shipment of the southern treasure to Spain, unless they were to be driven to the long, painful and very dangerous passage south around the Horn.

So Porto Bello had risen, or, rather, it was still rising. When the periagua passed the "Iron Castle" and stood away towards the town, Castle Gloria presented a complete outline. But there were moving lights on the sandbank where Fort Jeronimo stood and the sound of voices giving loud orders, and the noise of hammer on stone and on iron. Plainly, gangs of the slaves were being kept at work by day and by night. Forts Gloria and Jeronimo were now behind.

"We're past the teeth of the danger; we're inside the throat," said Louis d'Or. "Now, Tranquillo, tell us what we are to do next?"

"We can't risk a landing," said Kildare. "That is, of course we can't tie up at a wharf." He raised his head and sniffed the air.

"The tide is out. I can tell that by the stench of the mudflats," he said. "But the tide is at a stand, now, and it will be easy to keep the periagua drifting. With an oar-stroke now and then, you can hold her in place. So sail by the custom house quay and I'll slip ashore there. I'll be back inside an hour, I hope."

"Tranquillo," said the Irishman, "you've been in Porto Bello, they know your face, and wouldn't they rather put knives into you than into a good bit of venison?"

"They would," agreed Kildare, "but they think of me now as one of Henry Morgan's captains in boots and silks and lace and feathers and all that. They won't know the thing they see to-night."

He stripped off his clothes as he spoke, tousled his hair, and stood up naked except for a pair of short trunks. The sun brown of his body was almost as dark as that of an Indian. His hair was fully as shaggy.

And he had an Indian's body, also, slender, rounded and deep in the chest only, with never a bulky weight of muscle but only a swift ripple of strength here and there.

"Ay," said Louis d'Or, laughing, "if I found you like that, I might capture you and sell you for a slave even though you swore that you were my Brother of the Coast.—Go ashore then, Tranquillo. But I must go with you!"

"You will stay here," said Kildare.

"I'll go with you. No man can fight numbers, unless there is a second man to guard his back."

"I shall not fight," said Kildare. "Someone might be

scratched, here or there, but all they'll see will be the green of a cat's eyes and the flick of a cat's tail disappearing over a wall."

Louis d'Or and the Irishman began to laugh at this. In the middle of the laughter, Kildare listened for a moment to the noise of labor which pounded in Porto Bello by night, then he slipped into the water like a fish and went towards the quay of the custom house. When he reached the end of it, he could hear the bump and jangling of armed men walking their post, in military boots.

He simply worked his way a bit down the pier and then climbed out of the water. The sentinels with faultless regularity walked their post at the end of the wharf. They could report with perfect honesty that they had seen nothing. So could the inner guard at the side of the stone custom house. One of them heard a whisper, but whether of a voice or of bare feet, he could not tell.

While he was making up his mind, Kildare was safely in the long main street of Porto Bello. There were torches here and there to light the gangs of workmen. Some were clearing away the blackened ruins which had been left by Morgan's pirates. Others were laying stone or fitting great timbers in place.

And the rays of the torchlight flickered over the half-dried head, the tawny skin of Kildare and touched him with a fear as keen as the touch of fire. However, he got back through the twisting alleys until he reached the site of the house of Larretta, the big stone house of the rich merchant. There Kildare paused.

THE BUILDING WAS half-restored, and the work went forward now with a gang of a dozen negro slaves, under the

*Larrange held up both
hands for mercy*

eye of a foreman and a fiat-faced Spaniard whom Kildare
recognized as a clerk of Larretta. He would know, if any
man, whether Ines Heredia had been sent back to Porto
Bello and if so, where she was now in the town.

The clerk walked back and forth using a sheathed rapier
instead of a walking stick. Sometimes he paused to brush
at the mosquitoes which were eating him; sometimes he
groaned with weariness; but men who served that stern-

faced Larretta were not apt to forget their duty, whether by day or by night.

Near the torches of course there were more mosquitoes, gleaming clouds of them; so the clerk kept more to the darkness and it was easy for Kildare to come up behind him in the outer edge of the gloomy light thrown from the house. The noise of voices, of hammering, of pounding feet inside the house was ample to cover the softness of his approach. He pulled from inside his trunks that narrow-bladed little stiletto which was the small brother of his rapier, and touched the clerk on the shoulder, from behind.

"Pardon!" said Kildare.

The Spaniard, turning suddenly and angrily at the touch, saw the bare body and started to raise his sheathed sword to strike the impudent slave; then he saw the stiletto and stayed his hand; and as though by the glimmer of the bit of steel, he saw and recognized the man who confronted him.

"Tranquillo!" he cried.

But the cry was only a whisper.

Kildare touched his skin through the clothes with the needle point of the little weapon.

"Walk back with me into the darkness," he commanded.

His murmur taught the Spaniard to speak softly. "Will you murder me, *señor?*"

"You are as safe as though you were sitting at home with your family. Come!"

They drew back into the dark beneath a cedar which by the grace of a strange chance had not been consumed when the town burned.

"What is your name?"

"Larranaga."

"Larranaga, I am going to ask you a few questions. If you answer them truly, you are safe. If you lie, I stab you through the heart."

The Spaniard rested his body against the rough trunk of the tree. A weight of terror was bowing his legs.

"How long is it since you have seen the Señorita Ines?"

"Eight days, *señor.*"

The answer plucked a great, sounding string in the heart of Kildare.

"Where did you see her?"

"In Porto Bello, *señor.*"

"Where is she now in the town?"

"She is—she is living in rooms which her uncle secured for her, in the top of the custom house."

"Ah? That is a lie!" said Kildare.

THE CLERK FELL groveling on his knees and held up both his hands for mercy.

"*Señor,* you know the truth and I shall not attempt to deceive you. She is now in Panama, or nearing it if the mules are not lost in the horrible mud."

"Ah?" said Kildare, and a second stroke sounded in heart and in brain. "Why would they take her there?"

"Because they were afraid that Captain Tranquillo would never give her up, and that it would be best to take her from this unhealthy place to where there are so many soldiers—and where the buccaneers can never come."

"When did she start her journey?"

"Eight days ago, *señor,* I swear it."

"And you saw her?"

"Yes."

"Was she well?"

"Pale, *señor*, but calm and strong."

"Did you speak with her?"

"I only saluted her as she passed."

"Where will she be in the city of Panama?"

"In that place, also, there is a house belonging to Señor Larretta."

"Turn your face to the tree."

"In God's merciful name, *señor*—"

"Hush!" said Kildare. "I have promised to do you no harm."

With the man's own belt and other bits of his apparel, Kildare bound him firmly to the tree trunk and then gagged him, waiting until he could make sure that it remained possible for Larranaga to breathe.

Then he returned through the town. He was re-passing the custom house when he heard, out of the distance, a thin shouting that increased in volume, and then the beating hoofs of horses that flew down the harbor street. Crouched in a shadow, he heard men shouting. Their voices clashed together like violent echoes in a canon.

"Tranquillo! Guard yourselves! Tranquillo is here!—The pirate, the great pirate!—Tranquillo!"

And from the churches, bells began with an immense clamoring, rattling like brazen pans, beat against the ears of Kildare. Almost at once, a gun boomed from Fort Jeronimo, and he knew that the signal had been heard, the alarm had been spread.

And all this might have been avoided if he had rewarded Larranaga for his lie with one stroke of the stiletto!

He slipped over the side of the quay and dived far under the water, swimming hard until he was out of breath. He came up at a considerable distance from the quay, and looking back he saw men running along the length of it, looking vastly taller and darker than human.

Swimming straight and hard, he was quickly at the periagua and aboard it.

"The devil is up! Hear him howling," said Louis d'Or.

A small fishing boat was coming out from the dark of the shore, and inside it they could hear excited voices that rose above the increasing uproar from the town. "Tranquillo!" was the name, everywhere.

"Give way!" ordered Louis d'Or. "We are still in the throat of the beast, and nothing but luck will bring us out of it. Each man to a sweep. Oh, for twenty pairs of arms such as I have seen working on this boat!"

"This is all for my sake and my fault!" said Kildare.

"Your cause is our cause; your fault is our fault," said Louis d'Or. "Give way, men!"

9

THE SMOKE OF PANAMA

THEY PUSHED THE long, narrow boat ahead with wonderful speed. The sail was no help. There was not a breath of wind inside the flat bay of Porto Bello. And five men made a feeble crew for a periagua capable of holding thirty. Yet the great cedar log of which it had been built had been hollowed by fire and worked with the adze so skilfully that the remaining shell was both strong and very light, and the five sweeps pushed the periagua steadily onward.

A sound of many oars groaning against tholes came up behind them. They heard a command. Looking back, they saw the reaching prow of a long galley; the oars raised in a long row that gleamed in the starlight. Kildare could hear the water dripping swiftly and softly down as the great war-galley went by, with musketeers on her decked bows and more soldiers amidships.

Compared with the clumsiness of any sailing ship, such a vessel was like a spear to be taken in hand and hurled instantly at the enemy. The prow could tear a hole through the timbers of any ship; the single long, heavy cannon forward of amidships threw a shot of great weight, and the galley usually could be maneuvered so well and held so close to an enemy that a single shot from it might settle the fortunes of a battle.

So, with raised oars, the galley slid by them, and the frightful stench from the slaves on the galley benches wafted toward Kildare.

"Ahoy, periagua!" called a voice of hail.

"Ahoy, master," called Louis d'Or, changing his voice to a bawl.

"What are you?" came the imperious voice from the galley.

"Fishermen, master."

"Go fish at home."

"I cannot, master. Our nets are spread outside the harbor."

"Let the nets be damned."

"I will be damned by my wife if I don't gather the nets."

"Would you rather have a bullet through your hull?"

"Yes, master," said Louis d'Or.

At this, a great laughter came from the galley.

"Well, fool, go on!" said the voice of hail from the galley. "But do you know that Tranquillo, the great pirate, had been seen to-night in Porto Bello?"

"He will not wish to break his teeth on a dry bone like me," said Louis d'Or.

There was more laughter. The great galley dipped its oars and with one stroke shot past the periagua.

And they went on, neither trying to hug one shore or the other, but keeping well out in the center of the channel past the sandspit where the greatest of the forts stood, and so on toward the Iron Castle which was the first guard of the entrance.

They came so close that they could hear the voices of men at talk and at work at the fort. Then a sudden scream came from the periagua.

"Treason! Treason! Here is Tranquillo aboard!

There was a splash over the side. François, the mulatto, was overboard.

Instantly, from the fort, came sharp outcries.

Kildare drew himself up and shouted in good Spanish: "Watch the shore, pray! Runaway slave—swimming straight in—there is a reward! Watch to take him, friends!"

The instant answer came not from the shore but from the water.

"He lies! It is Tranquillo himself who speaks! It is the freebooter! Fire, Spaniards, if you want a great death to your honor! It is Tranquillo!"

"Pull harder! Pull harder!" groaned Louis d'Or. "The devil has undone us all unless we are quickly out of these narrows."

They pulled till their eyes started from their heads, but they were still close when a gun spoke in a deep, slow voice of thunder. They could see the flash of the piece, and then hear the plump of the solid shot into the water.

It had landed short of them. But other shots would be more accurate, surely. Every piece at the fort ought to have the ranges of the harbor entrance clearly marked. By starlight the task would be more difficult, but now the moon like a traitor was rising in the east and casting a white path always into the eyes of the periagua.

THEY STRAINED ON at the sweeps. The periagua, turned leaden, pulled back against their hands. Then four or five guns exploded in a single volley. Kildare heard a cracking noise, and turning, saw a clean hole drilled through both sides of the periagua, just a little above the water-line.

Then his face turned cool. A breeze was striking them.

"The sail! The sail!" he yelled, frantically.

They got it up by jerks and starts. More guns sounded. A wide hole and then another appeared in the cloth, letting through the pale eye of the moon.

But the breeze was taking hold. The periagua leaned suddenly far to the side as the wind put its shoulder into the sail. And they slipped away from the danger of the last fort. More guns were bellowing, leaving a long echo to roll behind the fugitives through the bay of Porto Bello. But every shot fell short and now the guns ceased, entirely. Only certain trumpet calls whined faintly in the distance as the periagua took to sea with a freshening wind off the land behind.

It should not have been so. The wind should have blown, after nightfall, from the land to the sea; instead the custom was reversed, and the narrow boat took full advantage of it.

A blunt-bowed round-ship came billowing out after them.

They held up closer to the wind and the round-ship fell behind them, letting off useless guns.

"We are free!" shouted the Irishman.

"We have only begun," answered Louis d'Or. "You see that shadow to the leeward of the ship?"

Kildare, at least, could mark it plainly. Long and low, it came shooting out from the harbor, bending sail after sail, square sails on the foremast, lateens on the main and mizzen—low, stumpy masts, but throwing out very long wings of canvas to catch the wind.

It was a galley, perhaps the very one which they had hailed inside the harbor. And that cloud of sail, catching the stiffness of the breeze, shot forward the slender haft of the galley as a hand shoots forward a javelin.

There was no question of escape through speed, for the periagua. Valiantly its single sail caught the breeze, at such a rate that rowing was of little use; but the superior sail-area of the galley flung it forward on the very arms of the wind.

"Clear the gun," said Kildare. "Are you ready? Clear it and turn it on the pivot, and God bless the man that put such a device in our hands."

Ordinarily, the periaguas could shoot their single pieces of ordnance straight forward only, aiming them with the turn of the ship's bows. This was a different matter, and they were able to pivot the heavy gun.

The periagua, in the meantime, fell off into the trough of the waves, and the galley came up like a running horse. It was clearly within easy cannon shot, but still it did not fire, counting on taking the stagger in little craft hand to hand, without the risk of sinking the prize.

"Let me!" said Luis the Mosquito Indian, as the cannon on the periagua was loaded.

"If he can shoot at all with the big gun," said Kildare, "he can use it as you or I could use a pistol. Let him have it!"

They stood to the sweeps, therefore, the three white men, while the Indian remained by the gun, screwing it into position.

At last he called: "Fall down!"

THEY DROPPED; THE gun boomed; white, stifling smoke swept aft into the nostrils of Kildare. He looked behind and saw the water lifted under the moon in a bright dash close to the bows of the pursuing galley. They were close enough to hear a shout of anger or fear from the galley. Frail as the periagua was, the galley was tenderly made for lightness and speed also, and one well-placed shot might smash it.

It gave to the port, then darted in again.

"Once more, Luis!" yelled Kildare, as he strained at a sweep.

And the Indian, after being frantically active at the loading of the piece, set it off again. The recoil knocked the periagua forward and well off its course. And from behind came a long, loud, endless yelling. A gun boomed from the galley, and the round shot ripped the air overhead, but even in those few moments, Kildare could hear the shouting from the galley diminish in force and volume.

He saw, then, that the foremost of the Spaniard had crashed by the board. The sail, trailing in the water, stopped all headway. The force of the wind in the after sails began to swing the craft helplessly around. Long sweeps were being put out again to right the course. Men poured forward over the foredeck to right the damage which had been done to the top-hamper.

"Sit down," said Kildare. "This is not the time for worry but for brandy! They will never continue this chase!"

The Spaniard did not follow. The periagua ran down the coast to the narrows of the isthmus and there landed. They found, as they had hoped, a small cove, and hove the periagua up into the mouth of a creek and there turned her upside down by the means of a good use of levers and tackle. They covered her, then, with green things. And then they held a council of war.

Kildare said to the Mosquito Indian: "Luis, we are going away for a long time. If you hunt up the Spaniards, they will be glad if you give them news about us. Do you hear? They will be glad to set a trap here for us, with the periagua as the bait, and fellows like the Spaniards will wait months to get such a prize as they think that we are."

The Indian answered: "Well, I have killed two Spaniards. I would rather kill one more than get from them everything that they can give. What have they? Only some yellow metal or some white metal and a man cannot eat that."

"You see?" said Louis d'Or, afterwards. "The man is a philosopher. He despises the goods of this world."

Their plans were very easily made. Luis the Indian would, he declared, be delighted to remain behind with the periagua. Its overturned hull gave him protection against the rain. Inside it were huge stores of powder and lead and guns and steel weapons of all kinds, and all that he needed to do was to see that the hull was covered with greens and that he struck enough fish every day to keep him in fresh food. This left the three white men to their own devices. And they took the shortest way through an argument by determining to follow the first stream up to the water divide and then down it toward the South Sea.

Each man took a musket, a supply of powder and lead, some bread, a flint and steel.

These were the physical affairs of their equipment. There were more important things, which they provided for with a brief set of rules.

One: If one falls ill, the two others will remain with him.

Two: If two fall ill, the third man will let them rot and go forward to accomplish the journey.

Three: He who grumbles at one meal shall cook the next.

Four: He who complains of any pain shall carry the muskets of both the other two during the next march.

Five: He who suggests turning back shall have no brandy for three days.

Six: In all matters, Captain Louis d'Or shall give the command, but where there is a difference of opinion a majority vote shall decide.

Seven: No Indians are to be killed, no matter how safe the killing may seem.

WHEN THEY HAD drawn up these rules, they plunged into the jungle.

That meant being wet from day to day, from dark to dawn.

At night they would kindle fires and try to dry themselves and their clothes, but, though the fires brought up a steam from the clothes and from the naked bodies of the men, no one ever was dry. The clothes were always wet. In the heat and the moisture the cloth began to rot. It tore with the putting off and the pulling on. To show what the moisture and the warmth would do, they came on a deserted Indian village where the coals of the last fires still were black, but the thatch, the huts and all their poles were already mildewed and turning green.

They handled the gunpowder like salt, drying it recklessly, close to the fires. But still their guns missed four times for every one when the powder would ignite. In the first two days they ate the last of their provisions.

In the next three days they had nothing whatever in their bellies except the river water. But they kept on, fixing their eyes before them, dragging themselves from point to point.

In the end, they would have to invade a large, armed town and try to fumble through a great church in their search for treasure, but no mention was made of the goal of the journey.

Spaniards were no longer terrible, as they marched through the steaming forest, sprouting with palms, hung with long beards of moss. All human beings seemed to them like brothers.

So they struggled forward, sometimes never speaking during the course of twenty-four hours.

All the time that their bodies were being assaulted by fever and weariness, their minds and spirits were being hammered and heated and rehammered into a finer sort of steel. They forgot the treasure which was their goal. Instead of treasure, they had for a purpose merely a goal. Towards it their wits and bodies were strained.

They reached the water-divide. They saw the waters of the streams beginning to slope down the way toward the great South Sea of Balboa. And then they could take greater steps, their knees buckling under their own weight.

In all of this, it was noticeable that the Irishman was the most enduring. Habit or nature kept a faint grin on his face. The sunburn left his nose. His face grew astonishingly pale.

Even his freckles became faint. But his spirit never wavered. Next to him stood Kildare—or perhaps even above him in sheer ability to march, seeing that his body was so light. Captain Louis d'Or suffered more than the other two. Having been in finery, he was now in the worst rags. But he made no comment until, at last, they came out of the western woods and saw before them not the outlines but the smoke of Panama.

10

POOR PEDRO

IT WAS A great town on the beach of the bay of Panama, built between the rivers Gallinero and Matasnillos. It was the greatest European city in the New World, perhaps, at this time. Seven thousand houses stood inside its limits. The great Spanish galleons were even in its harbor, unloading, refitting, loading to carry supplies to the rich south. Houses were built of native cedar or of fragrant rosewood, and some of stone, after the fashion of Grenada, the upper stories leaning out over the streets.

The cathedral of St. Anastasius was perhaps the most splendid building in the whole of the Americas, its great tower looking far out to sea, a landmark to sailors. And every stone was carved!

It was a city of merchants who lived rich lives, spending their hours and their money freely to forget the heat and the mosquitoes.

The King of Spain was strongly represented, with soldiers and with mules. The mules lived in long barracks, ready to carry the gold from Peru over the isthmus to the galleons which awaited the rich shipments in Porto Bello and other places. And there were two hundred storehouses of merchants with sheds sloping away from them for the sleeping quarters of the slaves.

It was a defensible city, because at high tide an arm of the sea put in across the savannahs and almost encircled the place; but on the whole Panama was defended not by forts but by its distance away from rovers, the impenetrable jungles of the isthmus being the living barrier between it and the danger from the buccaneer or other enemies.

The harbor was safe enough, but shallow. At low tide the long reach of mud stretched shining towards the sea; at high tide the southern houses might be invaded; because of this, ships did not land at piers, but were loaded and unloaded by means of tenders.

But it was a rich place, with gardens towards the landward side. Vegetables grew in squares and strips of well-manured land—manure was cheap from the king's stables. And there were guavas growing and alligator pears that taste like butter when they are fully ripe.

This was the greatest market in all the world for gold and silver, and perhaps no finer pearls ever were found than those fished out of the bay.

To the three fugitives, looking from the slopes over the green savannahs, past the pointed roofs of the old town, over the blue of the great bay, over the sweet green of the islands, and far away, the Andes gleamed like a distant and a gilded promise, a heavenly cool prospect in the far edge of the sky.

The three travelers looked at the view and they then pulled their belts more tightly about their gaunt waists. There was much work to be done, and talking was not the way to do it.

After that, they set forward along the road towards the town, a broad, straight road that grew better as they drew nearer and nearer to the smoke of the city which kept streaming up in clouds above the place. And every step, they knew, was taking them closer to a danger which might swallow them all, at a gulp.

They thought of the galley slavery, and said nothing; of the tortures of the Inquisition, and bit their teeth harder together.

All three were hunting treasure; one was hunting for the woman he loved. But in another sense none of them was hunting a thing except that other side of the world, that chance of throwing himself away which keeps men forever adventuring until the soul has died before the body.

They drew nearer, the size of the town reaching constantly wider and wider, pushing its roofs higher, the tower of the great church standing up like an angry arm, raised to warn them back.

Jogging hoofs and bells came up behind them. They saw a man running on his bare feet through the dust, beating a pair of donkeys before him, and they were loaded with flapping, squawking chickens, and with living kids.

The chickens were tied to the rear of the packs. Sometimes they flapped their wings wildly and tried to rise from their jolting perches. Sometimes they remained roosted. Sometimes they lost all balance of foot and of wing and hung at the length of the cords, head down. As for the young goats, a pair were slung over the bow of each saddle. Their feet were tied together, and so trussed, they were hung head down.

THEIR TONGUES LOLLED out. Their eyes were turning dim. Their bleating was uncertain and weak, but if they lived to the end of the journey they would be sold as fresh food, which was worth, in the heat of that climate, five times the value of meat slaughtered out of sight. No man, and hardly a woman, would trust the nose to declare what meat was safe and what was not. The Andes, after all, were much too far away to furnish snow for refrigeration purposes.

Here there was a thick grove of palms. And the three had halted in the shade. A rubbing with walnut juice, expressed from the bark of the nuts, had made them dark enough to pass as Spaniards or half-breeds. Their clothes were exactly as ragged as those of any of the poor of the land, and they all spoke Spanish like natives. So they were safe enough except for a close investigation.

Kildare, looking back at the approaching donkey-driver, murmured: "There is my passport into the town of Panama, friends."

"How?" asked the Irishman. "You wouldn't leave us, Tranquillo?"

Kildare sat down on the edge of the road, which was banked, and looked at his tired feet.

"Catch the man, bring him to me," he said.

When the half-breed came running up at his dogtrot, Padraic More took him by the nape of the neck and carried him to Kildare.

"Well done," said Kildare.

"The English!" moaned the half-breed, when he heard that speech, and fainted, so that he hung like a rag from the big hand of the Irishman.

Padraic More dropped him face down in the dust.

"Will he choke in the dust?" asked Kildare, leaning, curious, to watch the breathing of the fellow.

But little clouds of dust kept rising. The man still breathed regularly enough.

After a time he recovered himself and sat up. He sat on his heels and held out his hands, imploring.

"If you are going to eat me, my lords," he said, "kill me quickly. I am not a full-blooded Spaniard, and therefore my flesh will not taste better if you roast me alive."

"Do we eat the Spaniards after we have roasted them alive?" asked Louis d'Or.

"God and your noble lordships know the truth!" said the poor fellow.

"We only cook people who refuse to talk," said Kildare.

"Thank God I have learned to speak," said the half-breed.

"The truth?" asked Kildare.

"The naked truth, *señor!*"

Kildare took out his rapier and rubbed the blade of it until it shone.

"Take the goats off the saddles," he told the Irishman. And to the half-breed: "Why do you carry the goats head down, you dog?"

"*Señor,* but are they Christians?"

Kildare could not find an answer to that.

"You know the city of Panama?" he asked.

"As well as I know my two hands," said the other.

"You have heard of a rich merchant named Larretta?"

"Lordship, who but Pedro serves him with fresh goat twice a week?"

"Pedro, when were you last at his house?"

"Five days since, only."

"What was the talk there at that time?"

"The head cook has bought two new pigs to eat the garbage of the place. Better garbage than the new food that most of us eat!"

"Inside the house what was the talk?"

"Lordship, what am I to listen inside the walls of such a great house."

"PEDRO, YOU LISTEN everywhere. I know you. I see it in your flat eyes. What was the talk inside the house?"

"I only stood under the window for five minutes, and God defend me. I cannot tell how you knew!"

"And you heard what?"

"There are three great ships coming to Señor Larretta from the south coast."

"What else?"

"Some wine—"

"Damn the wine!"

"*Señor*, let it be damned. Let everything happen as you will."

"To whom did you hear Señor Larretta talking?"

"To a rich lady, *señor*."

"Ay, and what was her age?"

"She was very young."

"His wife?"

"He is not married, *señor*."

"His daughter?"

"I cannot tell."

"By what name did he call her."

"By the name of Ines, lordship. God forgive me if I have named the wrong name!"

He fell on his knees, for Kildare had taken a great breath and closed his eyes.

"Stand up," said Kildare.

The man rose.

"Where is the house of Larretta?"

"Above the wharfs, just above the mark that the water leaves at the highest tide."

"On what side?"

"You could never fail to find it. Let me show, you the way! No? Then you can tell it by its white face. And it is built with so much rosewood that your lordship could follow your nose to the place. It is to the southeastern part of the town."

"Tell me another thing."

"Everything that I know, lordship."

"There is a church of San Francisco?"

"Have I not prayed there?"

"Is there a peacock in the place?"

"In the church? God forgive me! *Señor,* Spanish churches are for Christians, not for beast or Englishm—" He clapped his hand over his mouth.

"Where is the church of San Francisco?" asked Kildare, suddenly smiling.

"It is the church with the two low towers, not a hundred steps from the house of Señor Larretta. *Señor,* let me show you the way!"

FOUR BLEATING KIDS, twenty croaking chickens, were a passport that brought Kildare readily into the town of Panama, even though he took the most guarded gate. The soldiers were too glad to have the noise away from them, and when the sun went down and the sudden, tropical

darkness poured like a black river over the city, windows
flew open and harsh voices cursed the racket which Kildare
carried with him through the streets.

In a way, it was as though he had carried a flaming torch
before his face, so that the Spaniards might recognize a
proved enemy.

But the greatness of the noise, on the other hand, was
like a smoke to obscure him. A pair of gentlemen on
muleback stopped to curse him—and then price a pair
of roosters. But he made no sale until he had reached the
depths of the town. There he put the poor, half-dead kids
on their feet, tethered the donkeys, and went to the house
of Larretta.

It was high tide. There was no smell off the mudflats,
now well covered, and the soft noise of the waves, coming
in through the shallow of the beach, kept the air pleas-
antly alive and brought a freshness of salty savor through
the hot town.

Kildare, wriggling his bare toes in the dust, stood watching the house of Larretta for a long time.

There was a wall around it. He climbed the wall, dropped
into a garden of flowers and palms, and with unhappy
thoughts of snakes and spiders in his mind, crossed the
damp ground to the inner wall. There he found the tall
side of the house, strongly built of stone below and of
wood above.

He rounded the wall until he heard the voices of women
and dropped on a bare knee to hear them more easily. One
voice had the harshness of Indian speech in it, the incurable
roughness with which Spanish comes off a foreign tongue.
The other was a gentler sound. He could not make out the

words it spoke, but he recognized the savor of the voice of
Ines Heredia.

Then he went up the wall like the cat he was. His sword
hung by a string inside his skirt and from around his neck,
so that it was a small burden. His dagger was inside his
trousers. And so he reached the window above, and hooked
his hard fingers over the ledge of it. There was a foothold
beneath on the rim between the stonework and the wood,
so that he could stand at ease.

"Tell my uncle that I am not going to dine with him. I
am not going to dine at all," said the girl.

There was another flow of protest.

"I shall not change my dress," said Ines Heredia, "because
I wish to be alone."

"But the *señor* has spoken a wish—"

"He speaks too many wishes," said Ines. "Leave me!"

The Indian woman puckered her face in spite. Already
she was composing the message which she would carry
back to the master. Then she turned away and left the room,
banging the door loudly behind her.

It was a big room into which Kildare peered. It was hung
around with that delicate Mexican featherwork which was
becoming a lost art, almost, and this kept a light whisper-
ing through the place, so that the sound seemed cool even
when there was hardly a breath of air.

The girl went to one lamp and put it out. She had gone to
the second and was leaning over it, her hair brightened to
a dim flame about her face, when Kildare spoke her name.

She started, but then came straight toward the window,
calling out in a hushed voice: "Ivor? Ivor?"

He slipped through the window. She tried to run and catch him in her arms, but he held up his hand.

"I'm covered with the street dust," he said. "If you touch me, you'll be marked, and that uncle of yours may come up at any moment to see you again."

"Take me away with you, Ivor!" she begged. "Take me now, before you have a chance to think again. But have you come alone into Panama?"

"I left some friends outside the walls. Stand closer to the light. There—that's better. Seeing you is better than drink. Better than food, also. I cannot take you away through the streets. But I'll come again."

"If you go and leave me, my brain will turn, Ivor. You've managed to come into the city once, but you'll never come again. My uncle has posted descriptions of you even here. He knew that you could not come to this place, but still he would take no chances, and the reward is published on your head, here."

"See for yourself," he answered. "If I take you into the street, you'll be seen."

"I'll make my skin dark, as you've done. How hideous you've made yourself, Ivor!"

"If you make your skin dark, still you won't walk like an Indian girl. And they have torches carried through the streets. I've come to see you not because I have a chance to carry you away, but to tell you that I'm here."

SHE SAT DOWN, suddenly, as though from weakness, and needing support. She wore a dress of the thinnest white linen with a tenuous robe of blue silk thrown over it; and there was enough of the sea-breeze through the window to give a life to her hair and to her garments. Kildare, staring constantly, felt his mind enriched and all his labors rewarded.

"Tell me what's happened," he said.

"Nothing. I was recognized on the ship. It belonged in fact to a friend of my uncle. And at Havana I was transhipped to Porto Bello, and then straight overland to Panama. That was all. My uncle still quakes when he thinks that you may find me again.

"And he shudders still more when he thinks that my fortune may slip out of his hands when I marry—even if I'm married to an Englishman. There is nothing else to tell, Ivor—only misery—waiting—despair of ever seeing you again. Talking doesn't help that. And you?"

He looked up at the ceiling, thinking.

"Well, I've found you," he said, "and that's all that matters. And I'm here looking at you—and have to leave once more. But God knows that this moment makes the world stand still! Is your uncle unkind?"

"He talks. But what is talking to me?"

"Is there a marriage in his mind?"

"Of course, but I smile at him. He tells me I am a traitor to my father and to him—but I still smile, and that makes him curse."

"I'm coming again," he said. "Not to-night. But if I reached you from the sea, with a boat in waiting out there—then that would be different? We could carry you off!"

"I have two feet that will carry me, Ivor. I don't need to be thought of like a bale of goods!"

They were silent.

"It's strange how calm we are," said Kildare. "My heart

beats as steadily as a clock. There isn't a leap along my blood. When I heard your voice I turned to stone—but now it seems as though you'd never left me."

"Because we both forget whatever went before loving each other," said the girl. "Everything else is silly and dull; like a thing we've dreamed and never lived."

Beneath the window, from the garden, a man's voice said: "This was the place. It was under this window."

And the voice of Larretta said, angrily: "This is the window of the room of my niece just above us. You say he climbed up from this place?"

"There was very little light. It looked like a mountain lion or a jaguar climbing, at first, but then his head turned, and I saw the face of a man—the paleness of a man's face—"

"Hallo!" shouted Larretta. "Jose! Ricardo! Antonio! Hallo! Thieves!"

Kildare waved his hand to the girl.

"What other way out?" he asked.

"There is no other way out."

She started to stand up, and fright dropped her back into her chair. Kildare walked straight past her, paused once to look into her face, and then went on through the doorway.

Larretta was crying, outside the house: "The room of the *señorita!* The room of Señorita Ines!"

KILDARE HEARD THE girl moan as he closed the door behind and shut himself into the dimness of an outer hall. Footfalls came rushing. He stepped inside the stiff folds of a great curtain and waited until the noises of panting and scuffing feet had gone by him. Then he moved again. They were up the stairs, beating at the girl's door. Her thin, steady voice was answering: "There is nothing wrong! I don't want you in here!"

Kildare smiled briefly, and went on down the hall. The steps wound to the left. They led him to a big, open hall, and across this to the main front entrance. The hurlyburly of the voices was all upstairs and in the garden.

So he picked up a big rug of fleecy goatskin, one of the huge skins of a mountain goat, wrapped a chair inside it, and with this apparently heavy burden on his shoulders, stooping, shuffling as though from the weight, he pulled open the heavy door, closed it behind him, and walked down the steps.

A squad of half a dozen soldiers came on the charge—so well was the house of Larretta guarded, so dear was he in the eyes of the authorities of the place. But they cast not so much as a glance at the peon under the high-built load. They bumped him aside and stormed on into the house.

Kildare turned into the street, dropped his load behind a hedge, and went back to his two donkeys. He turned loose the chickens in a cackling flight, let the goats stand where they were, and went on down the street, stepping in the soft thick of the dust, and leading the two weary animals behind him. For the sort of work that he still had to do this night, he wanted to make no noise, and the donkeys without any load on them would be recognized and serve as a passport to him when he wished to pass out through the gate of the town again, as he had entered.

In the meantime, he had seen Ines, he had the assurance worth more than gold, that she would be steadfast; and now he had to think of his two sworn brothers who waited for him outside the walls of the city of Panama.

On his left there were two blunt towers against the stars—the towers of the church of San Francisco, no doubt. He marked them, then hurried on.

The noise behind him had died out. Another in front of him began to grow, and as he turned a corner, he saw in a flare of marching torches two men chained heavily together.

A third man walked in front with the step of a conqueror. It was he that Kildare recognized first—the big head, the scrawny neck and shoulders of Pedro the donkey-man; and behind him, bloodstained, drooping, walked Louis d'Or and Padraic.

11

BLOODLESS CAPTURE

IF IT HAD been day, assuredly the crowd would have killed the prisoners; and certainly the soldiers who guarded them lifted not a hand to prevent the missiles which were flung. A gang of small boys ran naked or almost so beside the captives and threw at them clods of earth or whatever sticks they could find. A stone thrown in this manner had cut the head of Louis d'Or and caused the blood to stream down his face; but he strode along with a perfect unconcern as though he were unharmed.

And, as he went by, his glance turned piercingly through the darkness and found Kildare. He did not start or in any way indicate his recognition of a friend. Only with one hand he made a slight gesture whose meaning was clear: "Away—and save yourself!"

But Kildare followed in the crowd with the smoke of the torches blowing back about his face. The light made a tunnel through the darkness, an endless passage, and Kildare had a stifling sense of helplessness.

The procession reached the prison. It was a square-built chunk of stone, two stories high, with little iron-barred windows all around it; and a moment after the captives had been taken inside, a light glimmered in an upper casement.

Loud voices sounded from the same place, and the unmistakable sound of blows falling on flesh. Kildare bowed his head and leaned a hand against the wall of the building.

The crowd remained to cheer the capture of the English dogs for some time, but after a while it departed in a body, as though governed by a single will. Somewhere inside the jail an iron door closed and sent a long, harsh echo through the building; then there was stillness except for the sobbing of a woman on the first floor. Between sobs, she asked God to forgive her and let her die quickly. And Kildare gritted his teeth harder than before.

A pair of guards appeared around the corner of the building, the starlight glittering on their musket barrels. Kildare faded back into the darkness and let them pass, watched them come around again with a regular step. They, or others, would continue the march on the beat regularly until the morning. For a jail which contained English "dogs" needed special watching. That was clear.

As they turned the next corner the second time, Kildare ran to the wall. He had picked out his way beforehand, having noted that every fifth row of stones in the masonry projected a little. It was not a large projection in any case, but it was regular and it afforded a grip for fingertips, a purchase for toes.

He was halfway up the side of the wall when the regular marching step passed again beneath him. He was at the window of the cell he had marked out before the guards made the next round.

"Louis—Pat!" he called through the heavy iron bars.

He heard a clinking of chains.

"I'm here," said the guarded voice of Louis d'Or. "But

they've taken Pat to the torture. Tranquillo, have you turned yourself into a bird?"

"At least, I hope that I'll be able to pick a way out of the place for you, Louis." He was busily fumbling at the sockets of the iron bars. "They've used plenty of mortar to hold the bars; and if I can pick it out—"

He snapped the blade of his poniard. That left a short, stiff bit of the finest sort of steel, and with this he began to chip quietly, steadily at the mortar. It came away in the smallest of morsels until he had defined a small trench; after that he was able to break out larger and larger portions.

Half-sitting in the casement, half-clinging to the bars, he continued the chipping steadily. And beneath him, round after round, he heard the sentinels marching. If they looked up and saw the dark blotch of his outline against the stars—

Louis d'Or, inside the cell, was saying: "There is nothing that can be done! Why do you try, Tranquillo? Even if you get inside, the chains are bolted into the wall."

"But sunk with mortar around the head of the bolt; and I can chip that away as I'm chipping this."

"Go on, then, in the name of God. It isn't the dying that matters, but the way the devils will kill us. They're killing Pat now, I suppose. But an Irishman that locks his teeth on an idea is not apt to do much talking. They'll get no confession out of him, and without a confession they're not apt to put us through many steps to hell. A hangman's rope, and that's soon over."

"What happened to you?"

"THE SIMPLEST THING in the world. A troop of soldiers came down the road. We hid near it. I had a knife at the

throat of our chicken peddler to keep him from making
a noise, but he yelled out anyway, like a brave fool—and
somehow I hadn't the heart to cut his windpipe for him.
They took us. No use running from their horses. No use
fighting against twenty. We said that we were poor shipwrecked sailors. They said that all the English were shipwrecked as a rule and always poor, and generally pirates.
So they wrapped some iron chains around our necks and
took us away."

"You could have said that you were French."

"I said it and talked it," said the buccaneer, "but all white
men who are not Spanish are 'English,' in this part of the
world, and not to be trusted."

Kildare, having worked a deep trench around the base of
the iron bar, continued now to waggle the iron from side
to side. It moved very slightly, then with a greater motion,
loosening in its upper socket as well as the lower.

He stopped when he heard a sound of steps coming
down the hall. A key grated in the lock of the door, and
then it was flung open. Kildare, hanging by his hands from
the edge of the casement, peered over the sill and saw, by
lantern light, the huge bulk of the Irishman carried into
the room, his big head fallen over to one side, his mouth
agape, his eyes closed in death or insensibility.

They flung Padraic More down on his face and let him
lie. One of the jailers kicked the prostrate body. "English
swine, if I had had my way, I would have made you talk! I
would have made you describe the whole way to the hell
you're bound for!"

They went out and closed the door, calling over their

shoulders: "You that call yourself French—you hang to-morrow. May the knowing of it make you sleep better!"

Kildare pulled himself back into the casement.

"How is it with Padraic More?" he asked.

A groan from the floor answered him, and then a long-drawn, whimpering moan of agony. The complaint ended suddenly with a clicking sound of set teeth. Padraic More had returned to consciousness.

"How is it with you, Pat?" asked Louis d'Or. Then the big Frenchman said: "There's the third of us, brother, perched like a bird on the window and chipping the mortar to get the iron loose."

"Is it Tranquillo?" said the Irishman. "Ay, all the storms in hell would never keep him from a friend.—But he is not for me. Maybe I'll never walk again, Louis."

"What did they do?"

"I couldn't be talking about it," said More. "There's a taste in my mouth when I think of them, even. When I think of the Spaniards, there's a taste in the back of my mouth that won't come out till it's been washed clean with blood."

Kildare, with a sudden effort, wrenched out the bar. A bit of mortar fell, bounced from the sill, and sailed down into the darkness. He heard the spat of its fall against the ground. But the marching step of the guards had not yet turned the corner. Now Kildare was able to slide a leg through the gap in the bars and sit with a greater comfort as he attacked the second bar. His hand was sore from the work, but he knew the method of it, now, and even the starlight showed him in part where he was striking. The mortar came out more rapidly, as though it were softer at this place. To make amends for that advantage, he had to dig more deeply.

BUT THAT BAR, also, presently was loose at the base. He worked it back and forth in its socket as he had done with the first one. But the top stuck with a strange resolution. Using both hands, with a violent tug at last he broke it out with an effort that almost toppled him from his place. A good portion of the stone in which the top of the bar was set was also displaced in this manner and, though he caught at the falling fragment, it escaped from the tips of his fingers.

He looked down, with a groan in his throat, for the two guards had just turned the corner, and the fragment thudded solidly, exactly at their feet.

"Who's there?" called one.

And then a flash of fire, the boom of a report, echoing harsh and flat along the wall of the jail, and the impact of a leaden bullet close to Kildare.

"Turn out!" shouted the sentinels. "The English—they are breaking loose!"

Kildare slid through the gap he had made into the cell.

A sudden tumult had begun all through the building. There was an outcry from nearly every cell, and in the midst of it, Kildare, fingering his sword, knew that he was lost. He reached that judgment, and sighed.

"Out the window again, Tranquillo!" breathed the Irishman. "Out and take your chances on the wing. It's better to die fighting than to be hanged."

"There is no chance that way," said Kildare, calmly, "and the best way of dying always is with friends."

A moment later the door of the cell was thrown open,

and a bristling array of pikeheads and musket barrels and sword-points crowded the opening. The waver and dance of the lantern light struck wildly over the faces of the Spaniards.

A fellow in a short coat and a feathered hat on his head came in through the press, shouldering his way roughly. There was a certain nobility and even a beauty in his face, but it was as cold as stone.

"Ah?" he said. "Three instead of two? Two decoys have brought down the wild hawk, eh? What are you?"

"An Englishman," said Kildare, his sword in his hand but the point of it lowered.

"A poor shipwrecked mariner like the other pair?" asked the officer of the jail.

"I am whatever you choose to find me," said Kildare. "A dead man among other things, I suppose."

"Two of the bars are gone, captain," said one of the men.

"Did you do this?" asked the captain.

"With the point of a broken dagger."

"How did you reach the window?"

"By climbing."

"That is not—" began the Spaniard. But then he paused and stared fixedly at Kildare. "There are gentlemen in all countries, I suppose," he continued, still staring, "and brave men everywhere. Will you give me your sword?"

Kildare took it by the point and handed it over.

"It's more like a great needle than a sword," said the captain, "but a very swift hand could make lacework of men with heavy rapiers. *Señor,* you are English, and that is against you. You have broken into the prison of Panama. I respect your courage. The governor shall hear of you. But you will wait for his answer in that set of chains."

Kildare walked to the wall, where a heavy set of rusted irons lay on the floor.

"I am ready," he said.

The captain looked down at the sprawled, half-helpless form of the Irishman, who had raised his bulk on his elbows.

"If I had known that you had a friend of such a cut as this one—" said the captain, "well, it might have gone better for you."

Padraic More said nothing. He stared with a complete and childlike hate at the captain who suddenly turned and left the cell. An armorer was already fastening the chains on Kildare, and he murmured softly as he did so: "There are ten English scars on my body, dog! There shall be more than ten on you, in spite of the pretty talk of the young fool of a captain. This is a night to remember in Panama! Three English captured and not one drop of blood spilled!"

12

GALLEY SLAVES

IT WAS MID-MORNING of the next day when the door of
the cell was thrown open again and a pair of soldiers stood
on the threshold. Between them appeared Ines Heredia;
and the voice of the rich Larretta sounded behind her: "Do
you recognize any of them? Have you seen any one of the
scoundrels before, Ines?"

She looked straight into the face of Kildare and gave no
sign. Then she turned toward big Louis d'Or and the Irishman. She was shaking her head as she stepped back again.

"I don't know them," she said, with a perfect calmness.
"But why do you hang three strong men who could be used
in the galleys? In the galleys they die, also, but you have the
use of them. The galleys kill a negro in a year but you know
that an Englishman lasts for five times as long."

In the doorway appeared Larretta himself; Kildare
bowed his head, as though in despair.

"Two of them look strong enough," said Larretta, "but
the third one is a skinny wretch. However, since he's
English, we may be able to get work out of him. I think
I'll advise the governor to transfer them to the galleys. If
they hang, we have only a moment of pleasure. If they go
to the sweeps, we have years of use."

The door closed and was locked.

"She minds me more and more of my girl in Ireland," said Padraic More. "She looked at you, Louis d'Or, as though you were no more than steam out of the mouth of a kettle. And now she's giving us life in the galleys instead of death at the end of a rope!—But, Tranquillo, what would have happened if Larretta had seen *your* face?"

"The rack for all of us, and then the stake," said Kildare.

All Panama turned out to see the three Englishmen— for the complexion of Louis d'Or made him seem one of the hated Islanders—marched through the streets towards the wharf. And long howls of delight came from the crowd when More, who was scarcely able to walk after the torment he had endured only the day before, was helped forward with a whip. Luckily for him the walk was not long. By the wharf they found the galley, and looked down onto the squared superstructure where the slaves sat at the benches, three to a sweep, and twenty sweeps to a side.

Naked except for loin-cloths, sun-blistered and sun-blackened, they lay or sat in strange positions, striving to find attitudes of ease; for all were chained in place. The majority were negroes; Indians and half-breeds were few, being races of a weaker stamina and apt to die in a few weeks of despair and hopeless labor. But there was at least one man of northern blood, a fellow with long white hair, his body hunched by age as much as by toiling at the oar.

He seemed, in fact, far too old to be in the galleys, but over the hunch of his shoulders sprang two great cables of strength.

The galley was about to leave harbor for a cruise; sailors were busy with the top-hamper of the two big, stumpy masts, and the soldiers lolled on the platform forward. To the rear, under the canopy, stood the commander, the steersmen, and a fellow seated at a raised bench with a wooden gavel to beat the rhythm for the rowers.

At the edge of the wharf the clothes were being torn from the three recruits. They were marched not to a single bench, but each to a separate place, where old and practiced rowers would be able to show their duty to the newcomers. Kildare was chained in the middle between the brainless face of a great negro and that same old, white-headed man whom he had noticed from the wharf.

The sun already was beginning to sear his flesh and throw a lightness into his brain, when a man came up the central raised walk that ran the length of the galley and paused near Kildare. Fumes and heat poured from the charcoal brazier in his hand. Out of the brazier he drew something—a shadow moved over Kildare and then a thousand hornets stung his shoulder.

He heard the hiss of white-hot iron and smelled the singeing of his own flesh. That upward leap of Kildare, that yell that burst from his throat while his chains jangled, drawn taut, brought a loud chorus of laughter from the sailors and the marines of the fighting corps.

But the slaves uttered no sound as another man was branded and added to the life without hope. Negro and white, they looked straight ahead. Some of them shuddered a little, remembering, The man with the brazier went on. A loud curse from the Irishman told where he had gone; and then a phrase of snarling French proved that Louis d'Or had been branded in his turn with the tell-tale letter.

BUT A MOMENT later orders were being given, the ropes

were cast off and the galley put to sea. The commander, in full armor except for the head, stood under the canopy and spoke quietly. Beside him stood a boatswain who repeated the murmured order in a loud bellow.

The Spanish commander was the noble knight Pedro Alvarez and his nobility appeared most of all, perhaps, in the way his eyes overlooked the wretched slaves who rowed in his galley and concerned themselves only with the blue of the sea that expanded before the prow. He wore a narrow, delicately tapering beard and mustache to match; but the chief token of his dignity was in his armor. Whereas most nations preferred half or three-quarter armor, now that guns had been improved to such a point that a direct hit would smash a bullet through any sort of steel worn on the body, the Spaniards were apt to cling to the full fashion of complete plate; and Pedro Alvarez was equipped from head to heels in steel that was covered with golden chasings. And, sailor though he was, he did not fail to have on his heels a pair of gilded spurs. If anyone had told him that the costume was absurd, he would have replied that his father and his grandfather before him had been armed in exactly this manner and he had sufficiently good Castilian blood to prefer their ways.

The gavel of the rowing-master now began to beat, but Kildare was too rapt in his thoughts to pay much attention. The result was that something whistled briskly past his ears and a four-thonged whip fell on his back. Along the thongs were knotted bits of metal which cut into the flesh.

The heavy whip in itself delivered a blow of sickening weight, and afterwards Kildare could feel the warm running of the blood down his back. He glanced up and saw the broad-faced disciplinarian of the galley standing with a grin on his face and the whip raised for a second blow.

Kildare gave his weight to the handle of the big sweep and swallowed something in his throat that was colder than a stone and more bitter than brass. When he glanced towards the noble Pedro Alvarez a moment later, he could see that the proud gentleman, though still looking out to the blue of the sea, was smiling a little.

That smile left in the soul of Kildare a taste which never would quite leave him.

13

THE MUTE GALLEY SLAVE

AND YET, KNOWING that he was being initiated into hell, he found the fire a little less terrible than he had expected. For three days his skin cooked and swelled horribly though, after the first afternoon, he was given in common with some of the others a flat straw hat which saved his head and the top of his body a little.

The rest of him cooked, swelled, peeled, turned raw. Afterwards he began to blacken.

It was a season of little wind and sometimes an entire day passed and never once were the sails unfurled from the two long lateen yards—so long that they bent of their own weight at the ends. But when a good breeze blew up and all sail was made, then the slaves shipped their oars, for the narrow hull of the galley whipped through the sea like a flung spear through the air.

The days were the active torment; the nights were the seasons of despair, because then the cold ache entered the burns and sun-blisters and the fever which was not noticed during the heat of the sun entered the blood.

Hunger continually ripped the very vitals of Kildare. He was accustomed to long periods of privation at sea, but not combined with such labor. The captain of the galley had awarded to him a certain sum which was quite sufficient to feed the rowers well but, of course, the greatest portion of this money was a perquisite that passed into his pocket. Custom had established the exact amount of black bread and water that should keep a man alive and enable him, at the same time, to do a certain amount of hard work. And this ration was doled out, and no more. Few men could live on it indefinitely. A gross feeder might actually die of starvation inside two or three months and other men persisted in their endurance either because they were brutes incapable of forethought or because their well of nerve energy could be drawn upon to supply the needs of the body.

On the whole, there was a continual wastage. One could announce the length of time that men had been in the galley by the leanness of the ribs. The negroes altered in color, a dusty dryness appearing in their skin. Gradually a stoop appeared in the back of the galley slave. His chest caved in; his head began to thrust out; and the next symptom was a slight shuddering of the arms as the weight of the sweep came against the hands.

At that point the life of the man became less valuable to the captain of the galley than the cost of the bread which maintained him. On the second day out, Kildare was able to observe what happened in such a case.

The noble captain, every day just before the setting of the sun, walked down the raised platform that made the long backbone of the ship and actually lowered his eyes to the faces and the bodies of his slaves. His examination was quick but it was thorough. Something about Kildare having caught his eye, he spoke to his boatswain and the huge, flat-faced man took Kildare by the hair of the head

Armed to the teeth, they clambered up the side of the frigate

and bent his neck so that the captain could look straight down into his face.

Pedro Alvarez, as though contented with what he had seen, nodded and was about to walk on when something in the eyes of Kildare stopped him and brought him back. Whatever it was that he saw, the noble Alvarez suddenly lifted his hand as though he would strike the slave, but remembered in time that he must not soil himself by such a contact. The boatswain lifted his own burly fist and waited for the order before he flashed it into the face of Kildare, but the captain checked him.

"Let him be," he said, "because this is another man like the old white goat; this is one who will live thirty years in the galleys and never die!"

He went on, and a moment later Kildare heard a long,

quavering cry of terror. Then he heard the clanking of metal on metal, the pounding of the armorer as he hammered off the chains of one of the slaves. And now Kildare could see the poor negro crawling to the feet of the noble Alvarez, embracing his knees, yammering an appeal for life.

However, it was plain that the black man was almost spent. His bowed back never would quite come straight again; the vertebræ stood out one by one, like the knuckles on a great clenched fist. He was a skeleton, loosely draped in skin and the last few shreds of muscle.

HE WAS FLUNG over the side at once, straight in the path of the dorsal fin of a great shark. A great scream began, ended; and the galley continued on her way without losing the rhythm of the oars for an instant.

Kildare heard the noble captain murmur: "These waters will become safe for white men to bathe in; the sharks will become so used to black meat that they will take no other."

Captain Pedro Alvarez was wise enough to discard the slaves as soon as they were not worth the food they consumed. He was also wise enough to keep some degree of cleanliness along the crowded benches and on every Sabbath the sailors, with swabs and long-handled brushes, went the length of the galley and scrubbed down with sea water the naked six-score of the slaves.

The captain called this sweetening his ship. But in fact after the galley was a day at sea the noble Alvarez was compelled to burn incense under the canopy at the rear of the galley, whenever the wind was coming over the bows.

These cruises were not of very great duration because the fault of the galley—otherwise so maneuverable and efficient for fighting—was that its shallow hold could not contain enough food and water to support its crowd of fighters and its human machines for many days. But the galley was a splendid weapon for coast defense. And the noble Alvarez went out in three day circuits, from time to time, to search the waters for smugglers or, above all, for the dogs of English freebooters.

When they returned to Panama, after each trip the slaves were allowed to sleep on shore in a long, low shed. Sometimes, if they had had very arduous labor at sea, they were rewarded with a great pot of boiled maize in which a few scraps of salt meat or fat were thrown to give the mess a flavor.

And it was only during these brief moments on shore that Kildare had a chance to see either the Frenchman or the Irishman. There was never the slightest possibility of talk, but Kildare could see what was happening. The Irishman endured the terrible life well enough, but in ten days Louis d'Or looked like a starved wolf. It was perfectly plain that his high spirit could not live out the month.

Kildare himself lost, at once, every scruple of spare flesh, but after that he did not waste; he merely grew tougher and harder, like well-seasoned leather.

And, after a time, began almost to forget his own fate and that of his two friends, he was so engaged in studying the tall, white-headed, mute captive who worked at the oar beside him. The man's face was carved from wood. In his eyes there was a distant, dreaming look. And day by day he performed his labor in silence. Not once would he speak. It seemed clear that he did not know that Kildare was at his side.

It was a week before Kildare learned the incredible truth. The man had been forty years a galley-slave!

THE NOBLE PEDRO Alvarez had shown his skill in his selection of galley-slaves. Fully five of the six score who sat on benches in his ship were all of a single South African tribe, men who had been captured in battle with the whites not because they had surrendered but because they had been left helpless with wounds.

Alvarez had their heads cropped once a month and declared that he was the father of a shining family. They made their weight on the oars well felt when, on the third cruise, two weeks after Kildare had joined the galley, a sail was sighted and raised rapidly above the horizon with only a mild wind to help it forward. The galley, with the head sail set to help the oars, walked up on the stranger rapidly.

As the Spaniard came closer, it could be seen that the other was making the most frantic efforts to crowd on further sail, but the wind remained light and the game was clearly in the hands of Pedro Alvarez. Kildare saw him not only smile but laugh, saying to his boatswain: "English dogs! We shall have some new slaves at the oars before night; and only at the cost of a little powder and lead."

Therefore, he laid the galley under the windward quarter of the English ship and cleared his guns for action. There were three of them mounted forward, side by side on the rectangular platform; the central one of the three was comparatively a monster and it was plain that the little English ship carried no more than half a dozen cannon of small caliber.

However, he intended to fight, and now he fired. His broadside of three shots fell harmlessly into the sea, far short of the galley. The noble Alvarez laughed again, before he put on his heavy steel helmet.

He gave orders. The big forward gun spoke and sent a shot well beyond the Englishman. It spoke again and still overshot the mark, so Pedro Alvarez had the gunner lashed to the mainmast and flogged thoroughly. A second gunner landed a pair of bullets far from the target, also; and in his turn he was triced up into the rigging and whipped till he screamed. But the third man had better luck. With his second discharge he brought the foremast of the enemy tumbling down and the Englishman fell away from the wind and lay almost helpless.

Pedro Alvarez forgot his gentility in a wild burst of exultation. He ordered a closer position to be taken, still to the windward of the English. With his greater range of cannon, he now stood off at a convenient distance and slowly hammered the foreigner to pieces.

Kildare, his heart swelling, saw the lost men of the little ship cut away the wreckage of their foremast; he heard their deep-throated cheer as they loosed another volley at the Spaniard, all the shots falling far short again. Two of the guns on the port side were silenced. The third still continued to pop uselessly away; and still with each round fired the English cheered. Their flag remained dropping at the masthead; there was not the slightest sign that they intended to strike. And Pedro Alvarez continued to laugh, with raised visor.

His gunners, having the perfect range, then silenced the third gun on the port side. It was now possible to come straight in, particularly when another shot brought down the mainmast of the little ship with a crash.

And Pedro Alvarez ordered the Englishman to be rammed; and while the ram was still buried in the hull, the marines and sailors were to board and capture the prize.

That should be an easy task. The total crew of the little ship was not apt to be more than a score; and on the galley there were three times that number of soldiers and sailors. The dragging mass of the mainmast, moreover, made it impossible for the Englishman to maneuver to escape from the ram. The ship lay helpless while the galley, with a groan and creaking of the great sweeps and a soft rushing of water down the sides, ran in to give the death stroke.

KILDARE HEARD THE orders given by the noble Alvarez to load the three bowguns with small shot and musketballs. At pointblank range the three were discharged with a shock of recoil that staggered the galley from end to end. And Kildare, glancing back over his shoulder, saw that a mere scattering of three or four of the English appeared behind the nettings which had been strung up along the side. His heart sank. Even the ramming of the little ship seemed a folly. The Spaniard had only to range alongside and throw a prize crew aboard a helpless prize!

Then, solidly, heavily, with a deep crunching of metal through wood, the galley struck its prow into the side of its enemy. The impact swayed Kildare far back; it toppled many of the slaves off the benches and threw them into a wild confusion for a moment.

The moment the blow had gone home, the whole mass of the fighting Spaniards delivered a crashing volley of small arms and swarmed forward for the hand-to-hand attack. The noble Alvarez moved not to lead them but to accompany the attack, holding his long cut-and-thrust rapier straight upwards. He was now in complete armor, his visor down, looking like a metal monster.

There was not an instant rush from the galley onto the Englishman, however. The marines and sailors, armed to the teeth, were clambering up the side of the frigate, yelling furious insults and death to the English dogs, but those dogs still were managing to show some teeth.

Kildare, twisting about, saw that to the assistance of the three or four unwounded a dozen bleeding wretches had staggered to the rail and now were fighting like madmen— or Englishmen.

They fired muskets and pistols; they thrust long pikes down through the boarding-nettings of tough, tar-boiled rope; and where a rent had been hacked by the Spaniards in the nettings, and half a dozen of them were struggling to press up onto the deck, yonder stood a single big-shouldered man who already ran blood from half a dozen wounds.

He had tied a rag about his head to keep the blood from a scalp wound from blinding him, and with a big double-bitted axe in his hands he rapped the Spaniards over their helmeted heads or sank the blades so deep into their flesh that they tumbled back faster than they could climb up.

The noble Alvarez, enraged by this delay, began to lay on his own men with the flat of his sword, cursing them for cowards. And while the English captain, armed with the axe, cheered on his men and forgot his own wounds, the Spaniard from the rear kicked his men into the fight.

One elderly, grizzled tar on the Englishman, suddenly hurled into the galley some small hammers and a number of cold chisels, shouting: "There you, black devils! Free yourself and then help us!"

Both a hammer and a chisel dropped within the reach of Kildare and he had them instantly in his grasp. It took a bit of skill to apply the edge of the chisel to the overlapping edges of the steel manacle that fastened on his legs but presently he sprung it apart and with a stroke or two in the same way liberated the old white-headed slave beside him. Rapidly, gaining skill each moment, he continued that work, springing the manacles of man after man. He half expected them to leap instantly into the fight, but to his surprise, they sat like stunned men.

If he could get to Padraic More and Louis d'Or he would find a different response, but they were not close to him. **THE SPANISH CAPTAIN** now began to shout to back water and haul the galley out of the side of the Englishman. They had received a bloody nose instead of an easy conquest and the idea now was to stand off at short range and blow the English from their decks with small shot from the guns.

The captain himself ran back from the prow down the central walk of the galley to take command from the stern, and it was at that moment that he saw the mischief which was being worked among the crew of his slaves.

For Kildare, crawling under benches like a wriggling snake, had reached More at last and with quick blows of hammer and of chisel was liberating the powerful Irishman. And Padraic More was mumbling: "Quick, Tranquillo! I want to die. I only want to die, if I can have one taste of Spanish blood before I knock under!"

The shackle, in fact, dropped away as the noble Alvarez,

with a great shout, turned on them and raised the bright
length of his sword.

And they were unarmed. Except for the few hammers
and chisels which the English carpenter had flung down
into the galley, there was not a sign of a weapon for the
slaves. And most of the blacks, even those who already had
been liberated, sat stupidly, as though they had not the
slightest idea of what to do with freedom.

So Kildare turned, with only that short-handled, light
hammer in his hand, and the chisel; very feeble weapons
against a man in complete armor with a good Spanish
blade in his grip and the bearing of one who knows how
to use it.

And as the captain shouted in rage and made his stroke,
Kildare held up the short, thick chisel to catch the edge
of the blade. The shock almost knocked the chisel from
his grasp. The glancing force of the sword descended on a
chained slave on the next bench and wounded him beneath
the neck and the shoulder horribly and deeply, so that a
great spout of blood leaped up into the air.

But Kildare was on the central walk of the galley by
that time. As the noble Alvarez drew back his sword for a
second blow, the short hammer rang once and again on his
helmet, putting two deep dents in the side of it. Alvarez
fell on his knees, and Kildare snatched from the numbed
fingers that beautiful and well-balanced length of Toledo
steel.

The yelled orders of the captain before he fell in that
moment, had started half the slaves to work on the sweeps,
and the galley, after a sway to this side and then to that,

finally was backing away from the Englishman, followed by a wild cheer of derision and triumph from the sea-dogs.

But here the marines and sailors, hurrying back from the prow where they had been trying to board the Englishman, found Kildare in the center of the walk, swaying the long, bright sword like one who is a master of weapons.

A far more terrible sight appeared the next moment.

That old, white-headed English slave who had spent forty years in the galley, had run straight back to the helmsman and had throttled him with his bare hands. Then, picking up the heavy box of cutlasses and long sea-knives which stood unlocked on the after-platform, he now carried it forward and cast it down among the blacks. Those who were free leaped to the prize like birds from the air stooping at food on the ground.

THE CONFUSION WAS now absolute pandemonium. More of those chisels and hammers which the English carpenter had flung aboard were being used by the black men to help themselves to freedom, for at last they seemed to understand the example which Kildare had set for them.

Those that were free were instantly armed with cutlass or knife. And from every throat came screeching sounds such as never could issue from civilized throats, and queer, high-pitched whining phrases which last had been heard in the battle in some African jungle.

The Spaniards, their captain gone and that wild confusion before them, hesitated for a moment and in that moment they were lost. Their lieutenant began to shout to them to charge forward but while they delayed an instant Kildare ran on down the raised walk, shouting, waving that long, borrowed sword.

If the Negroes could not understand his words, his action was perfectly clear. The blacks leaped to follow him. And here at his side was huge Padraic More, brandishing a cutlass, laughing with a huge joy.

And yonder a tall man leaped high up from among the benches. That was gaunt Louis d'Or, lean as a wolf, and more savage now than ever a wolf was. He, too, had steel in his hand.

With More and Kildare, he made the front rank of the charge that struck against the Spaniards. A pistol exploded in the face of Kildare, scalding one cheek and setting fire to his hair, but the bullet missed him and he put the point of his sword through the throat of the marine. More and Louis d'Or each brought down a man. And then the blacks came in.

They came like mad beasts. If they could not get past their white leaders, at least they could get around them. The rigging was to them no more than jungle trailers to apes of Africa, They ran along the gunwales to get in on the flanks of the Spaniards. Climbing high through the rigging, they dropped down like fighting cats; and the steel claws with which they scratched dug deep into life.

There was no end of them. Those who remained at the benches were liberating one another rapidly and rushing to join the battle. Some of them were too eager to hunt for a weapon but went in with hands and teeth.

And Kildare saw one black, with a pike thrust clean through his body, actually fasten his teeth in the throat of a marine—and topple overboard.

Kildare, beating out the flame in his hair with one hand, now drew back from the mêlée.

He was in time to see the noble Alvarez, armor and all, hurled overboard by two slaves; but Kildare made no effort to rescue the knight. He was studying the last stand of the Spaniards in the bows of the galley. For they were fighting men, as brave as any in the world on land but always ill at ease at sea. They showed their clumsiness now by trying to form ranks as though they were on a parade ground, but the tide of blacks literally closed over them. For every armored Spaniard there were two stabbing, snarling blacks.

Those who tried to stand shoulder to shoulder either were brought down with wounds and then murdered as they lay on the deck or else pushed overboard; and armored men cannot swim.

There were, besides, the sharks. They had plenty of blood to draw them to the spot, and now the sea was alive with dorsal fins that cut the waves like black scythes.

The time of the terrible outcries was very brief. Then came a silence, a swirl of reddened water, and only the deep, infrequent groan of a hurt man, sick with his wounds. **KILDARE HAD BEEN** in many a wild fight, but this, the moment it was ended, seemed to him to have been an explosion, a rending of the air with a great sound; and now as an after effect there remained a red, slippery deck, the horrible, nightmare heads of the sharks lifting from the waves every moment with mouths agape, blindly feeling into the blood-drenched water for solid food; and near at hand the negroes looking at one another with gaping mouths of laughter and rolling eyes.

One other thing happened, then. Or, rather, it dawned at last upon the mind of Kildare. It was a cheer from the little English ship which had given occasion for the moment of liberation to all the slaves. It was sinking rapidly, now, down by the head and heeling far to port.

And into a small boat the living survivors were descending. A wretched half dozen of them, and every man of these stained from wounds. And still the sea-dogs cheered in spite of their pain!

From that picture Kildare looked back at the galley. A grey-headed black-man with a good deal of dignity in his bearing now came up to him and, kneeling, uttered a few indecipherable words and taking the hand of Kildare laid it on his head. The negroes very plainly agreed to this act of submission with one very violent and cheerful cry.

Kildare looked from them towards one bowed, white-headed form. That was the old English slave. He was more red than white, now, because he had been in the thick of the fight; but he had resumed his place at a sweep as though he had never left the galley bench, and he waited for further orders with his old hands hooked about the thick neck of the oar.

14

THE TRAIL TO PANAMA!

THE GOOD GALLEY "Santa Magdalena," late in the service of His Majesty the King of Spain and now in the service of a hundred African negroes and nine or ten white men, lay on the white of a beach near the mouth of a lagoon. In the top of a great palm that stood well out on the beach was posted a lookout, for the ships of Spain were busily sailing in search of the fugitives and an armed force might come upon them.

However, only rough weather would drive the galley in from the open water, and in smooth waves they could laugh at the fastest of sails. They remained in readiness, as they lolled on the shore, to remove the stays that held up the galley and run the light ship swiftly down into the water as soon as any formidable stranger appeared. After that, coasting along the inlets, they could easily escape from a strong force or else capture a weaker one.

It was the same crew which had washed the galley with blood and cleared out the Spanish masters of it but it never could have been recognized. Cruising gaily here and there, they had overtaken a number of the little coastwise trading frigates which plied between the Isthmus and the rich ports of South America. The pillage of those vessels had

been carried into the galley—as much, at least, as could
be used. The result was an ample provisioning of everything one could desire, from munitions of war to food, and
including a great quantity of European finery which had
been trans-shipped from Panama for Peru. In these clothes
the negroes delighted and wore them now on the beach as
they took their leisure. The heat—and their own fancy—
prevented them from wearing more than one garment at
a time, as a rule.

It was all Kildare could do to keep them from trying the
keenness of their new weapons on every Spaniard taken
out of a captured frigate. He had been forced into the
command of the "Santa Magdalena" with or against his will
because the negroes had accepted him, after the battle, as
the originator of the plan which brought them liberty and
they called him their king. As Louis d'Or pointed out very
clearly, with such a force at their command they might well
hope to run in on one of the great treasure galleons beating up from Peru and take it, after nightfall, with a sudden
rush. So both negroes and whites had been cruising with an
infinite relish. Each black man felt that he was already rich.
There was at this very moment, for instance, a great kettle
of pork and sweet potatoes stewing on the beach, and the
former slaves to go to it to eat whenever they chose. This,
surely, was to be rich. And as for the white men, they lived
in the expectation of finding riches.

It was about this expectation that they talked on this
morning, all of them in a close group except Kildare, who
walked moodily up and down, trying the weight and the
fine balance of the blade which had been just finished for
him by the blacksmith. It was made of a remnant of the

beautiful Toledo sword of the noble Alvarez and was of exactly the proportions of that other weapon which he had lost at the prison in Panama. At his belt, besides, he carried another slender needle of a stiletto. So he was equipped in his former fashion, but his heart was not greatly raised.

THIS WAS POINTED out by Bartholomew, the captain of the English. He had sailed from Plymouth with more than eighty men in two small ships. Disease and the terrible weather off the Horn had cut down his party of hunters after Spanish treasure to the handful which remained when Alvarez came up in the galley. This Bartholomew was a very wise fellow, but all of his front teeth had been knocked out years before in a fight and he talked with a foolish lisp. He still had not quite recovered from his wounds in the recent battle, but his spirit was high.

"That Tranquillo," he said, "is a mysterious fellow. Not long ago he had a brand on his shoulder, an oar in his hand, and only a year or so of labor before him until he was dry of juice and thrown to the sharks; and yet he walks up and down like a king who has been driven out of a kingdom."

The Irishman explained, briefly: "He wants his girl. And she's in the hands of her Spanish uncle in Panama."

Bartholomew whistled; then he lighted his pipe and consoled himself with smoke. "Well," he said, "they're wearing black on his account in Panama now; so the girl won't be forgetting him."

Kildare, stopping in his walk, stared at the bright blue-gray of the sea and then turned and regarded the face of the jungle which rose like a vast green cliff, flowering into gold and crimson at the top, while an entangled curtain of lianas trailed down like a waterfall.

And he felt that he was imprisoned between Western Ocean and the jungle.

He came back to the council of the whites and stood over them, the smallest man by far of them all but with a keen, bright temper of mind and soul that made him their master—unless it were for the Frenchman, Louis d'Or.

Kildare said: "Panama is the treasure-chest. How shall it be cracked open?"

"What!" cried Bartholomew. "Are you thinking that a handful of men like this can sack the great city of Panama, with thirty thousand people inside it, and ten of them able to carry weapons?"

"If we can't do it—why," said Kildare, "if I can't break a thing with my hand, I get a hammer and try again. What's the hammer that we could use? Think for me, Bartholomew—Louis d'Or—all of you!"

Louis d'Or said, thoughtfully; "If the King of France sent his Marshal Turenne with thirty thousand men to the eastern coast of the Isthmus, not twelve thousand of the men would get through the jungle to Panama, and those twelve thousand would be so weak from the march that the Spaniards would sweep them away and murder them all. Remember, Tranquillo, that your Spaniard who doesn't know what to do with himself at sea, is a good two-handed fighting man on dry land."

Kildare held up his head and drew in a great breath.

"If men can't take Panama," he said, "then what can be done?"

"Nothing can be done," declared Louis d'Or. "You might steal the lady, brother, but you'll never take her by force. Men won't be able to rush the walls of Panama."

"Men can't do it?" echoed Kildare. "Well, buccaneers are not men. They're devils, and they can live on gunpowder and a good chew of lead."

"Where will you get the buccaneers, Tranquillo?" asked Bartholomew.

"I can't tell," answered Kildare. "Think for me, all of you. Who can raise a flag that an army of buccaneers will follow?"

"Morgan! Admiral Henry Morgan, as they call him now!" said Louis d'Or.

"Morgan? That is true," pondered Kildare. "But he hates me with a good, cold, long-lasting hatred."

"He hates nothing he can turn into money. Show him a trail to a profit and he'll forgive you," said Bartholomew. "I know Morgan well. I knew him before he was famous. I knew him in London."

"Show him a trail? I shall!" exclaimed Kildare. "I'll show him the trail to Panama!"

AFTERWARDS, THEY SAW Ivor Kildare sitting by himself, moodily, in the shadow of a palm tree, his head in his hand. And when they were ready to put to sea again, about noon in the day, they found not Kildare, under that tree, but a letter from him, which said:

> *Dear Louis and Padraic,*
>
> *I have gone. You will not be able to find me. Stay here with the Santa Magdalena and make your voyage. Already you have picked up a good bit of the Dew of Heaven. There is more of it ready to fall into your hands.*
>
> *I am going to try to come back, but not alone. If you hear of strange doings off the east coast and a mustering of ship and men,*

perhaps I'll be among them.

If you ask why I am leaving you, I reply that one man can travel faster than three. Three are not enough to fight off the Indians or the Spaniards, but three are surer to be seen. That is why I have chosen to go alone.

If you hear of me no more, I beg you, Louis, to write a letter to my lady in Panama. But this is an unhappy thing to think about. Happiness will come to us, after all I am going to get the hammer which will crack open the treasure-chest.

Adieu.

Ivor Kildare to you both; but burn this before the rest discover that I am not the cutthroat Tranquillo, and so lose my old rating with them.

Louis d'Or, standing as one stunned, slowly read out this letter to the English, omitting only the portion after the signature.

"Search for him!" shouted Padraic More. "Call the blacks! Tell them their king has left them in the lurch!"

"You cannot find him," said Louis d'Or, "any more than you can find a jaguar in the jungle without dogs to catch the trail. He is gone as surely as though he had dived into the sea. As for the negroes, they'll follow me, I think, and that is the thought of Tranquillo, also."

"Ah hai!" cried Padraic More. "To be without him is like being without fishing gear, when the rivers are filled with fish."

15

CAPTAIN MORGAN

HOLLOW-CHEEKED, HIS RIBS sticking out like raised fingers, his clothes mildewing on his back, Kildare came out of the jungle on the eastern shore and went up the coast to a little inlet. At the mouth of it he paused and shouted until the place rang: "Luis! Luis! *Ah hai!* Luis, my friend!"

He waited. There was no answer. He shouted again and still again without result, and then, turning because of a sudden coldness which had gripped the small of his back, he saw the tall Mosquito Indian standing just at his back. The face was as old, as dour as ever, but he had been true to his trust and had remained there through the weeks with the periagua.

Kildare took his hand with a hearty grip.

The boat was in good order. Luis had seen to that and he also had cleverly patched the two holes which the Spanish cannonball had knocked through the cedar sides of the craft, using rounds of wood and cementing them in place with layers of resin. With long wooden levers they turned the periagua on its keel and worked it by degrees down into the water.

It was not easy to handle a boat of that size unless the

weather were favorable, and Luis shook his head as he looked up and down the length of it.

"Where are the others?"

"On the farther side of the land," said Kildare. "Luis, you've won your freedom from me. You can go back to your home now, if you wish."

Luis shook his head.

"On shore, it is good to be single, but it is bad for a man to be alone at sea. I go with you."

He got out a sweep and began to pole the long boat down the inlet towards the open, blue water beyond.

CAPTAIN HENRY MORGAN—"ADMIRAL" he was more often called now—sat not many days later in his own private room of his own favorite tavern in Port Royal. Out the window he could see a palm tree, a bit of white beach, and half a dozen ships riding at anchor in the haven. So long as the captain could see blue water and ships riding on it, he felt as a miser feels when he sees gold, because by ships and sea, Morgan was on the trail of fortune.

He was at ease in mind because of the loot of Porto Bello and the other Dew of Heaven which he had gathered here and there. He was at ease because his was the greatest name and fame that ever had come to any buccaneer since the jolly tribe of cutthroats and pirates had begun to ravage the Spanish mainland around the shores of the Caribbean Sea.

Now he indulged himself in a period of repose during which he soaked his body daily with excellent brandy punch and gave over his mind to dreams of midnight assaults, flame, shoutings, the sound of guns—and at last the breaking open of treasure chests. He was now cracking nuts and eating them with a relish, dipping them in salt to keep alive his thirst for the brandy punch.

For every two nuts he ate himself, he tossed a third to the expectant paws of an ape which sat on a chair on the opposite side of the table holding himself up like a caricature of a man. And now, into the moment of this perfect repose, charged thundering feet on the stairs and a voice that shouted: "Captain! Captain Morgan! Oh, Captain Morgan?"

"Here, Saunders, you bawling, blundering jackass!" called the great Morgan.

Through the door burst a big, red-faced man with three or four pistols thrust into his broad sash and a heavy sword to accompany them.

"You've been fighting," said Morgan; "there's blood on your jacket."

"It's the luck of the devil that keeps me from being dead," gasped Saunders.

The ape, disturbed by this interruption, hopped onto the table and thence onto the broad shoulder of the captain, where it sat up moving its long upper lip to clear the fragments of nuts from its teeth.

SAUNDERS DROPPED DOWN into the vacant chair and helped himself to a long pull at the punch bowl. The eye of Morgan measured the amount of disappearing liquor with a grim interest.

"There was Tucker and the Swede with me," said Saunders, when he caught his breath again. "We took him on the run. Tucker from one side, and the Swede from the other, and I came right in from the front. And Tucker went down like a stuck pig with a thrust through the thigh. The

Swede's face is ripped open and he's blind with his own blood. But I got only a prick through the sword arm that made me drop the blade, I tried to pull out a pistol and finish him that way, but the point of his sword was right at my throat. He told me to take myself off and tell you he is coming."

"Who? Who is coming, halfwit?" demanded the captain.

"Tranquillo!" breathed Saunders. "The moment we saw him, we rushed in—"

Henry Morgan pulled a pistol out of his belt and laid it on the table.

"Were you drunk, the three of you?"

"Sober, by my oath!"

"And he took the points of all three of you and laid you out in a row?"

"You've seen him dance in and out when he fights?" groaned Saunders. "Well, he was dancing that same measure to-day. Where you thought to put your sword right through the flesh to the bone, there was nothing found but thin air. And then a glitter in your eyes—and the damned sword like a touch of witchcraft—"

"He said that he was coming to me?" demanded Morgan.

"He did."

"Jimmy," said the buccaneer, "what's best to do?"

The ape reached down and picked a nut off the table and put it into his mouth. After that he began to tousle and gently scratch the head of his master.

"Jimmy Green says for us to stay right here and carry on with the nuts and the punch," said Henry Morgan. "Saunders, get three or four more and watch the stairs. Have Wilkinson, that praying murderer of a Wilkinson, come to watch my door. If Tranquillo says that he will come to visit me, he'll come—And if I fail to catch him, my name is not—"

"Henry Morgan," said a voice outside the open door, and Kildare stood on the threshold.

Henry Morgan, slowly lifting his pistol, aimed it straight at the breast of his visitor. Big Saunders gave back a pace as he snatched out his dagger and the length of his rapier. The edges screeched against the scabbard in the haste of the draw.

But Kildare, in a ragged shirt and tattered breeches, his feet bare, and dust more than ankle-high on his legs, bowed to the captain, and his black hair fell forward a bit over his face as he made the courtly gesture.

"You see, Morgan," he said, "that two good men are apt to have a need of one another. I've come to talk."

He sat down in the chair which Saunders had just left and picked up a clean cup, which he filled with the punch, and tasted the drink.

"Too strong!" he said. "Too strong, Morgan. You are going to die happy and rich—but young."

SAUNDERS SLIPPED AROUND until he stood at the back of Kildare. And Morgan, his fleshy brow wrinkling, his eyes beginning to bulge with the fury of excessive hate, tried to speak, but only made a grimace.

"Saunders," said Kildare, "stand away from my chair because you keep off the sun. Your captain knows that I would never have dared to come to him unless I had a treasure to pay for my safety. Morgan, send the red-faced hulk out of the room—and order a bottle of Madeira for me.

I don't want to scald my throat with your fire and lemon juice, there."

Morgan began to breathe like a winded horse, loudly, through a flare of nostrils.

But at last he said, huskily: "Jimmy Green, damn you, what would you do?"

The ape reached for another nut and cracked it between his teeth. And at this, Morgan suddenly laughed.

"Jimmy says you should have your own way," he interpreted. "Saunders, get out and send up the Madeira. Now, Tranquillo—or Kildare—or whatever sort of a name fits a five-footed hunting cat like yourself, tell me how you are going to pay for that Madeira?"

"I am going to make you rich," said Kildare. "And famous."

"I'm famous already," said Morgan, "but damn fame. I prefer pieces of eight."

"I am talking about them. And good Peruvian brandy by the tun."

"Well?"

"Mexican gold and silver work by the mule-load."

"Ah?" said Morgan, leaning forward.

But the ape, incommoded by this change of attitude, squeaked a protest and secured his balance by gripping the hair of the captain. Henry Morgan, obediently, leaned back in his chair again.

Kildare continued: "Warehouses filled with silks and laces and bales of gold cloth. And gold bars. Enough to load a train of mules. That's not all. There is a warehouse where the silver is piled up like cord-wood, seven feet high in a room thirty feet long."

Morgan groaned.

"Thirty feet long?"

"Yes," said Kildare.

"Where?"

"Panama."

"It will stay there, then, and you know it."

"It would stay there except for one thing."

"What is that?"

"That is the brave Henry Morgan."

"Tranquillo, there are thirty thousand people in Panama."

"There are five thousand buccaneer devils sailing the Caribbean, who want nothing except to follow Henry Morgan."

"The city's fortified, I say."

"The walls are old. The forts are poorly armed."

"The way to Panama is the way to hell."

"There's no easy way to the Dew of Heaven."

"Get out of my sight, fool!" shouted Henry Morgan.

KILDARE LAUGHED, AND the bottle of Madeira was brought in by a frightened servant who looked with popping eyes at one of these famous men and then at the other.

"You are sweating, captain," said Kildare.

"Such fool's talk would make any man sweat."

"Thirty feet of silver bars, piled seven feet high, like firewood," said Kildare.

"My God," said Henry Morgan, "what a beautiful thing even to dream of."

"What a thing to pack into the hold of a ship!"

"Such a raid would cause war; I'd have the English navy about my shoulders."

"One part in a hundred of the loot would be enough to buy the courtier who has the king's ear."

Morgan frowned impatiently.

"Tranquillo, be silent! Shall I go mad? Shall I lose my sleep forever, thinking of this?"

"Not if you sail for the Main with five thousand buccaneers."

"There would be no way to take Panama by surprise. The jungle is filled with Indian spies and they would carry the warning. The whole city would be under arms long before we came. Every man and boy in the city would be practicing with muskets."

"Muskets fired by children can't kill buccaneers."

"As for the treasure," shouted Morgan, "the governor would ship it south from the city for safety."

"All the better," said Kildare. "Our ship lies in wait and picks up the crumbs that fall from the table when the great Henry Morgan sits down to eat the city."

"Tranquillo—madman! What ship have I in the South Sea?"

"I have one."

"Impossible!"

"A ship with a crew of a hundred and ten fighting men."

"In the South Sea?"

"Yes, in that sea."

"You dream, Tranquillo."

"The ship is there. The good galley 'Santa Magdalena' with a crew of ten English and a hundred negroes of the fighting sort—men of iron, Morgan. Men who have been hardened by the labor in the galleys until bullets would glance from their bodies. Men who laugh when they fight."

"Galley slaves?" said Henry Morgan.

"I've told you the truth. A hundred and ten men armed with pistols, muskets, light and heavy cannon, knives, swords, and a very neat new device—cutlass blades mounted on pike staves for the Africans to use."

Henry Morgan was silent, staring. Tempted.

"Five thousand of the right sort, red and raw, men who love the Dew of Heaven and jolly Captain Morgan. They'll run across the Isthmus-like so many rats over a granary floor. They'll scamper into Panama. They'll raise the fame of Captain Morgan like a smoke between earth and heaven."

"Wait!" exclaimed Morgan.

"I'll wait. But not your men once they know the great idea. Why, Panama is the treasure house of the Western world. The king of Spain is wakened every morning by singing girls, and all they sing is 'Panama! Panama!' When he looks at his crown jewels he touches the biggest diamond of them all and says: 'Panama!'

"If you have Panama, you have cut the throat of Spain and all the wealth of the south country bleeds into your hands. Henry Morgan will become a name that will echo between the sea and the sky like the gallop of a horse down an empty street on a frosty morning."

"A ship?" said Henry Morgan. "A ship already in the South Sea?"

"It is there."

"With a hundred and ten fighting men?"

"I've told you that. As good men as you'll ever find for the sacking of Panama."

"Tranquillo, it was not very long ago that you were

running away from me like a rabbit from greyhounds. And now you tell me that you have a Spanish galley on the South Sea, ready to capture the birds that I flush out of the Panama brush?"

"I tell you all that."

"Then," said Morgan, leaning back with a groan of relief, "then you lie!"

"You wonder how I could get my hands on such things, Morgan?"

"Yes, I wonder."

"See for yourself!"

He snatched off his ragged shirt and turned. On the flesh of his shoulder the big scar was incised, for the white-hot iron had devoured meat as well as skin.

Henry Morgan rose slowly from his chair, still staring.

"Ah?" he murmured at last. "Ah?—Then you are one of the devils who eat fire and digest it. Tranquillo—do you hear? I believe everything. We'll go—we'll leave only a scar where Panama is standing to-day!"

16

A ROYAL COMMISSION

AS FAST AS the fleet frigates or the smoothly sliding periaguas could carry the word, it sped across the Caribbean to every port where wild sailors might be found, willing to turn freebooter; and to all the word was given that Tortuga was the rendezvous.

Most of all the messages flew to Hispaniola where the buccaneers by the score were following the trade which had given them their name and boucaning the meat of wild boars and half-wild cattle in the woods of the great island.

And the name of Morgan was a trumpet that few could fail to hear after Porto Bello and Maracaibo. His was the call and the summons was reinforced by all that ever had been seen or heard of Spanish treasure.

These bright visions filled the minds of the adventurers who gathered swiftly at Tortuga where their admiral waited for them in a tall Spanish ship which he had plundered from the enemy in one of his recent raids.

A party detailed to the de la Hacha River returned with a shipload of grain and thousand sacks of maize in addition, and a great quantity of jewels from the pearl-beds. With this for provender, the fleet would not quickly starve. Almost better than the surety of food was the news which

"Admiral" Henry Morgan read aloud to an assemblage of his captains who had gathered on his flagship in the Tortuga roadstead.

It was a very curious paper such as never had been in the hands of a buccaneer before this day and it had been secured after a long session in which Captain Henry Morgan in boots and splendor and Ivor Kildare in the rags he had brought from the Isthmus, sat with no less than the Royal Council of Jamaica province, in the town of Kingston.

For a few words which Kildare had heard from the lips of the late noble Alvarez were now sufficient to bring a great reward. The Spaniard had said, on a day, to his lieutenant, that it would not be long before many more galley-benches were filled with English dogs; because preparations were under full weigh to start an expedition to attack the English and drive them from Jamaica into the sea; it would have been equipped and it would have sailed long before, except for Henry Morgan's sacking of Porto Bello.

The rags of "Tranquillo" and the hollows which were still in his sunburned cheeks gave a conviction and a force to his words. The Royal Council, straightway, commissioned Captain Henry Morgan to act in the name of His Majesty, Charles the Second of England, to carry war into the territory of the hostile Spaniards, wherever they might be found in force. The buccaneers, when they heard of this commission, first laughed and cheered, and then cheered without any laughter, because they realized that this important paper might secure them from death on the end of a hangman's rope, if they were captured.

It was at this meeting that the rules were published. To
Captain Henry Morgan went one share in every hundred
of what the expedition captured. To every captain, four
shares unless his crew voted him more. To every lieutenant,
two shares. To each ordinary man, one share.

No plunder would be allotted until the wounded had
been proportionately compensated.

There were certain special provisions. He who pulled
down a Spanish standard received fifty pieces of eight.
And a surgeon got two hundred pieces for his chest of
medicines. A carpenter for his tools, one hundred pieces.

Any captain who, with his single ship, captured a Spanish ship at sea, should receive, with his crew, one-tenth of
her value.

THERE WERE NOW, in the roadstead of Tortuga, thir-
ty-seven ships carrying well over five hundred cannon.
Outside of sailors and boys, there were two thousand
musketeers. The total number had not come up to the
prophecy which Kildare had made to the famous buccaneer, but at least there were upwards of three thousand
trained and hardy ruffians assembled for this greatest of
all the buccaneer expeditions.

And so, at last, sails were hoisted, and the ships went
down the sea to Cape Tiburon, where a great cargo of
oranges was taken aboard, a special value attaching to them
for the prevention of scurvy. After that, they bore away for
the mainland.

It was up the River Chagres that they intended to push
into the land; that meant, first of all, a necessary attack on
the fort at the mouth of the river, and since the place was
strong there should have been more misgivings about even

the initial step of the expedition, but when the buccaneers looked at the assemblage of their craft, when they thought of the luck of their commander, they were ready to laugh at all dangers.

Towards Chagres they sailed, therefore. And Ivor Kildare on a starry evening sat on the high poop of Morgan's ship with the admiral in person beside him. The helmsman behind them was a sober fellow and chosen for that purpose. He had had one eye knocked out by the Spaniards and he was lacking a large part of his face because a Spanish bullet had passed through it; but he drank neither rum nor brandy and therefore he was of great value in a crew like that of Morgan's.

Down in the waist, up in the forecastle, by small lantern light the buccaneers ate and drank and danced and gambled and fought. There was hardly a moment when high, snarling voices were not being raised on one part of the deck, while singing amused others, and now and again a pirate inspired by a drink or by a lucky winning at dice would go leaping and dancing down the deck. Impromptu musicians with various instruments were always tuning up to play new airs that made a conflicting jargon with one another.

Kildare, sitting cross-legged beside the high admiral of the fleet, with his chin on his fist studied the riot on the deck. Henry Morgan, beside him, sipped brandy punch from a big bowl, as usual, and looked from the riot below to the queer, hunch-backed figure of Jimmy Green, the ape, who was amusing himself by running up the flag standard until he could swing from that frail rope to the mizzen topmast shrouds.

"What do you gain from this, Tranquillo?" asked Henry

Morgan. "You beat the drum that starts the idea marching in my brain; you argue the Royal Council—the block-
heads—into giving me a royal commission for stealing; you
offer yourself to guide us through that hell's tangle of the
Isthmus; you bring us to the gate of the town of Panama;
best of all, you promise to bring up your ship from the
South Sea to hover around the port and catch the birds of
rich plumage that try to run away from the town; but what
do you gain? Come, come, you can't tell me that it's all for
hatred of the Spaniards or for the love of Henry Morgan
that you'll do this?"

"Inside the town," said Kildare, "there are two things that
I wish to find. One of them is Ines Heredia."

MORGAN WHISTLED. "ARE you still running around the
world after her like a little dog after its master?" he asked.
"Make a queen of a woman and she'll make a slave of *you*."

Kildare said nothing. Morgan went on: "For a man like
Captain Tranquillo, Port Royal is full of pretty wenches,
and any one of them, in a month, can make you as sick of
women as the high-headed Spanish lady will make you
in a year."

Kildare looked up at the shadowy swelling of the big
square sail just above them and said nothing.

Morgan returned to the charge: "Well, I'll try to keep
all hands away from her after Panama falls."

"I'll be the first to her," said Kildare, quietly.

He looked Morgan in the eye, and the admiral turned
his head slowly away and seemed to be smiling a little.

There was a whisper, a thumping of a rope overhead, and
Jimmy Green appeared above them, hanging head down.
Morgan stared for a long moment at the ape.

"Tell me what's in my mind, Tranquillo," he said.

"You're wishing," said Kildare, "that when the fighting's over you could wash every buccaneer from your decks and sail home to Port Royal with a crew of monkeys."

Morgan laughed.

"They'd make no more noise than the drunken apes on the deck, there," he said.

"And they could be paid off with nuts and bananas instead of pieces of eight," said Kildare.

Morgan glanced at his companion again. "D'you know the trouble with yourself?" he asked.

"Tell me," said Kildare.

"You're one of those damned romantics," said Morgan. "Except for that, I'd make you my vice-admiral and put your flag at the mast-head of any ship you wanted in the whole fleet. Look at me, now. I'm a practical man. A pipe of tobacco and a bowl of brandy punch makes me at home in any country in the world.

"You throw away a treasure for the sake of a woman's smile. And you will never be at home until your feet are on green turf again, with an English skylark in the middle of heaven, and your own chosen lady walking on your arm. The page of your life is all margin, Tranquillo, and damned little writing on it to call your own!"

17

WITH GUNS PRIMED

AFTER ALL, FOR the sake of securing the safety of his men in the rear and getting more provisions, Morgan touched at Santa Catalina Island, first, and summoned the governor to surrender the two forts. The governor returned word that he knew he could not contend against such an armada, but he begged to have a mock attack made so that his honor might be saved. This was done.

The buccaneers, with much laughter and yelling, fired their guns into the air and the defenders furiously loaded and discharged their cannon without charges of bullets.

Afterwards, there was a mock attack from which the Spaniards fell back; and a little later they surrendered.

This easy victory was taken as an augury for the success of the entire expedition. That savage sea-dog, Captain Brodely, was then sent with a division of the fleet down the coast to that place where the Chagres River rushes past a steep hill into the Caribbean; and on the steep hill stood the great castle of San Lorenzo, guarding Chagres harbor whose twenty feet of water made a good harbor for all except the largest ships.

Captain Brodely landed a league below the town, marched overland through the swamps, and came up behind San Lorenzo fort. Three hundred and fourteen soldiers defended the place. And there were perhaps four hundred buccaneers outside the walls. They would never have taken the place, which was defended by a true Spanish hero. But when a night attack was being driven vainly against the palisades of the outer defenses, a buccaneer in the ditch was struck in the back by an arrow. He jerked it out in a rage, wrapped some cotton around the slender shaft to fit it into the barrel of his musket, and then fired the arrow furiously back at the Spaniards. The cotton adhering to the arrow caught fire from the exploding powder and, landing in some woodwork, set it presently in a blaze. Other buccaneers followed the example of that chance and soon the whole place was in a blaze.

But the heroic Spaniards still defended the earthworks all that night. The next day they were charged and retreated into the ruins of the inner fort, where the noble governor was shot through the brain. Then thirty of his followers, all that remained of the three hundred except a few who had slipped away in a small boat up the Chagres to carry the warning to Panama, surrendered. Of the buccaneers, half were dead or wounded. It had been a glorious defense and chance had won the battle almost more than courage.

News of this success started Morgan forward again. He blew the Spanish forts into the air at Santa Catalina, and sailed to Chagres. It was a very joyous entry into the harbor, and the whole fleet broke into a great cheering when they saw the English colors that flew from the earthen walls of famous Fort San Lorenzo.

Morgan, laughing very cheerfully on the deck of his flagship, told Kildare that he had pulled one of the biggest teeth out of the mouth of the King of Spain. In fact, he had done so.

But the first of many troubles now came on the expedition. For the buccaneers were standing about the rum keg or the brandy cask in every ship drinking healths to King Charles, Admiral Morgan, and to one another. And so the leading ships grossly missed the way into the river and, with a freshening norther behind them, four were grounded on the rock ledge of the entrance. The great ship of Morgan was among them.

The guns which had been firing salutes were silenced at once; the cheering ended; the whole harbor was filled with activity. Some tried laboriously to warp the ships off the reef, but the gathering force of the norther began to break them up, and therefore the four vessels were emptied and stripped of all useful goods. After that, they broke up on the reef under the gloomy eyes of Henry Morgan.

HE WAS A man who could not be downhearted for very long, however, and he started at once to repair Fort San Lorenzo, because as long as it was in his hands his retreat from Panama would be secured. The captives taken from Santa Catalina, together with those from Chagres, were set to work building and thatching huts, sinking new, strong rows of palisades to top off the earthen walls of the fort.

In the meantime the preparations for the plunge into the jungle went forward. Five hundred men were left as a garrison in the castle and two hundred more to hold the ships of the anchorage. That left a scant twelve hundred for the journey to Panama, for sickness, desertion, wounds, and death had whittled down the handsome army with which Henry Morgan left the roadstead of Tortuga. Kildare

Henry Morgan proved himself no ordinary pirate

urged Morgan eagerly to leave a mere handful to watch
the mouth of the Chagres because, as he said:

"You have not seen the walls of Panama!"

Morgan was obdurate. "With nothing else to show King
Charles," he said, "I'll still have San Lorenzo and Chagres,
and in London they pay high for captured fortresses, Tranquillo. They give out titles. They make men knights and
barons, Tranquillo, for just such feathers as San Lorenzo
to stick in the hat."

He scratched the back of Jimmy Green as he spoke, and
Kildare stared at him in amazement; that brandy-stained,
brandy-puffed face aspiring to a baronetcy was something
too strange for smiling; and all the murders, cruelties,
cheats, and robberies of Henry Morgan came storming
through the mind of Kildare. However, the end was to tell
whether or no the ambitions of Henry Morgan were so
entirely absurd!

For the overland trip, Kildare suggested plenty of food supplies, even if the army had to labor along with an annoying slowness, but Morgan was all for a flying trip. He knew that the Spaniards, having been warned of his coming long before, might very well ambush him in great numbers somewhere among the jungles of the Chagres, but he said this was all the better. He would kick the Spaniards out of his path and his army would live on food taken from the enemy.

SO THEY MADE the start in thirty canoes or periaguas and a few of little chatas, which were shallow-draft boats specially intended for work along the rivers. Kildare, with Luis the Mosquito Indian, took charge of the leading boat, which was a chata with some light brass and iron guns on board.

He sailed with the guns primed and the matches lighted because at any moment a storm of shot and Indian arrows might be poured upon them from an ambush; but in fact by dark they had covered six leagues against the current before they anchored at De los Bracas.

It was an excellent beginning. It was a stride so long that the buccaneers talked as though they were already in Panama. But Kildare was a gloomy man. They had taken with them only a small store of maize and a few strips of charqui for each man. And the reckless buccaneers, instead of keeping the provender and using it very sparingly, devoured most of the corn and the jerked meat on that first night for their supper because, they said, they had to feed their bodies if their bodies had to feed the clouds of mosquitoes. Along the shore at De los Bracas there were a number of plantations, but the Spaniards and their slaves had run away and left nothing but bare huts behind them.

They went on the next day with the thin, maddening song of the mosquitoes continually about their ears. It was very hot, and since this was January—the dry season—the river had fallen low, with stretches of black, stinking mud often on either side of the stream.

The rapid jungle green was already sweeping over these newly exposed flats. Trees lay wedged in the current, big trees that had been swept down by the floods, and these had to be cut or dragged out of the way.

Once the prow of Kildare's chata bumped on a living log, and from under its keel slithered a mud-colored crocodile. Kildare bounced a bullet or two off its armored back and sent the chata on.

His heart was sinking all the while, and his faith in the success of the expedition was at a very low ebb. The men had for the most part eaten nothing but tobacco smoke during the day. And an empty belly is a poor friend in the middle of a jungle with the night coming on.

When the dark came, the multitudinous singing of the mosquitoes was the undersong, and the chorus above it was composed of the cursing of the starved buccaneers.

They cursed Henry Morgan to his face and that night Kildare sat for a long council with the leader. Luis, the Mosquito Indian, sat with his sour, old face at that conference. He told Morgan that the boats could be dragged or rowed another six miles up the stream.

MORGAN SIPPED BRANDY and then rubbed some of the strong liquor on his face and hands, which were badly swollen from the poison of the mosquitoes. He looked purple-red and his eyes were swollen so that he could open them only as slits of light.

"I was wrong," he said to Kildare. "I should have taken more food along. But who would have thought that the Spaniards would run away from us and let us sink this far into their land without once rallying to strike us? Tranquillo, we should be eating the stew cooked in Spanish pots, to-night. Instead, we eat air! The dogs should have stayed to fight us and let us have their fare. They are too cowardly wise!"

"I can take a picked crew and a few of the best and lightest boats and be back here in three days with enough provisions to last all the way to Panama—if the men eat sparingly," said Kildare.

"They will *not* eat sparingly," said Morgan. "If food comes now, the beasts will bolt it and turn themselves sick; and that will mean a fourth day of halt, while the mosquitoes drink up our courage and leave an itch in its place. No, no, Tranquillo! Look at Jimmy Green. He tells us that the worst thing an army can do is to turn back. He points us forward."

The monkey, in fact, had fallen asleep with his head on the knee of the admiral and one outstretched, hairy arm pointing up the stream of the Chagres!

So Kildare lay down, at last, to try to sleep. But the mosquitoes prevented that with their songs and their poisoned lances.

18

RETURN TO THE BOATS

THEY LEFT THE boats behind them the next morning because another day of labor at the oars would reduce the entire army to exhaustion and despair and it seemed better to cut a way overland, with Kildare to point the road.

A hundred and sixty men were detailed by Henry Morgan to guard the boats, so bringing down the strength of the force to little more than an even thousand. But the retreat would be secured in case of defeat and a remnant of the beaten host getting as far as the Chagres.

The last injunctions of Morgan to the boat crews were by no means to leave the boats and go ashore, no matter in how strong a party or how well armed. For through the deep sea of the jungle, Spanish spies might creep to within scant yards of foragers and pick them off. So the grim little army left that planter's station of Cruz de Juan Gallego and entered the woods.

Kildare, as guide, selected a force of strong macheteros to hew the way through the jungle. It was a long, green tunnel which the machetes opened, as the steel blades were humming and swishing through the juicy green stuff. Very pale, because the sun never had touched much of this growth, at times the tunnel became almost as white as a greenish ivory.

And slimy, crawling things moved out of the way; and always the thick, rank stench of the jungle fumes was in their nostrils, while the horrible woodticks dropped down to the scent of blood and drank life far more deeply than the mosquitoes could do. "The devil himself invented the garrapados!" said Luis, and he took a soft ball of wax and rubbed it over the skin of Kildare, the small ticks sticking to the stuff and the bigger ones being brushed off. Also, a waxed skin offered a more difficult surface for the pests to catch on with the barbed hooks of their hind legs.

It was the stifling air that made the men begin to drop. Half of them, presently, were either prostrate or down on one knee, breathing hard, turning pale. And Morgan had to lead them back to the boats.

It was a bitter decision. He muttered to Kildare: "This is the first backward step, and probably it is the end of the expedition. God curse the day when you tempted me to it in Port Royal!"

That day they rowed, poled or dragged the boats to a miserable bivouac at Cedro Bueno—a name rather than a place. And now the men were chewing bark, grass, and any sort of spicy leaves that they could find—chewing them because the rank juices allayed the belly torment a little. This was the night when a score of the buccaneers headed by one Samkin Butterworth, a hump-backed man famous for his strength, came to Morgan and insisted that the expedition should return; it would be impossible to reach Panama.

Kildare never forgot that scene with the smoke of the

bivouac fire rolling over Morgan and himself, keeping the mosquitoes away but nearly stifling the men.

"We'll ask Jimmy Green," said Morgan, speaking only from one side of his face, the other being now too painfully swollen by the mosquito poison.

But Jimmy Green was busy picking off ticks and killing them with his vicious, sharp little teeth.

"You see," said Morgan, "that Jimmy says it is better to kill deserters than to leave them behind us for the Spaniards: to pick up and torture information out of 'em. So the answer is, Samkin, that if you try to leave the camp I'll have you followed and thrown to the fish, by God! Now, get out of my sight, you rotten piece of tick-food!"

The last words came out with a tremendous roar. Samkin hesitated only a moment, and then turned and led his companions away in a rapid flight from the wrath of the admiral.

Henry Morgan, stroking the monkey, grinned at Kildare.

"What would I do without Jimmy Green?" he asked.

IN THE NARROWER stream above Cedro Bueno there was more water and the boats made a slightly easier progress. Even famine, as the hungry bellies of the men shrank, became easier to endure. And besides, they caught a few fish, most of them struck by the instinct and the uncanny skill of Luis the Mosquito. He followed Kildare always close at heel, silently, day and night, with a face sour as vinegar and darker than thunder, but with a nameless devotion in his heart.

They were climbing out of the deeper jungle. It was easier to march along the shore and on the fourth day of

the journey most of the men took to the land, with Kildare
as their guide, the rest following in the canoes.

On this day it was that a sudden thickening of the green
ahead of them drew suspicion, and then they were able to
make out an irregular breastwork of felled trees. Plainly
the Spaniards had built an ambuscade and the buccaneers
might have suffered fearfully from gunfire in front of it. But
the only thought of these men, when they saw the fortifi-
cation in the forest, was that where enemies lurked, food
would be found, also. So they charged with yells of joy, but
after all the place was vacated long before. The first sight
of the unshaven savages from the Caribbean had been too
much for the Spanish stomachs, or perhaps the tale of the
winning of Fort San Lorenzo now weighed heavily on
their minds.

At any rate, the buccaneers found not an enemy, not a
scrap of food, except bread crumbs and crusts which had
been trodden into the ground, with some leather bags also.
Those leather bags were torn to shreds and chewed to a
pulp and swallowed.

They spent the night at Torna Munni and marched on
through the heat, the mosquitoes, the blood-sucking ticks,
and at noon of the fifth day—nearly four days of starvation, now—they came with weak knees into the little town
of Barbacoas.

But the Spaniards had even uprooted the crops lest the
buccaneers should find sustenance, and the village was bare
of everything that could be eaten except that in a recess in
the rocks were found two great sacks of ground corn meal,
and two large jars of wine. It would have gone down the
gullets of the first to find it, but Morgan ran when he heard

the joyous howling and beat the finders from their loot. That nourishment was given only to the men who were palpably dying of starvation; and many a life was saved by that act of good management.

Kildare, for the first time since the march began, was able to render a hearty admiration to his leader. It had been fine generalship. It was an act so wise that even the most savage of the buccaneers had to admit its excellence.

That night they spent in a bean field from which the Spaniards had removed every trace of sustenance again.

The sixth day was hell on earth.

From chewing grass and bark, a brown or a green crust appeared on the lips of the men; the same lips were cracked and bleeding; and Henry Morgan stalked with the rear guard, his face now a hideous blotched distortion but his resolution growing more gigantic with every step he took.

He kept with him the strongest men in the army and with these he picked up the men who had fainted. Some of them were beaten forward; some were carried; none were left for the Spanish spies to pick up and torture. One man in ten was now going ahead on hands and knees. Those who had friends, sworn-brothers of the Coast, frequently were seen arm in arm, staggering on and giving one another a strange mutual support. The affection between them seemed to serve instead of food, to some degree.

BUT HENRY MORGAN retained the strength of his idea, and Kildare, though he was a bundle of wires and bones, was sustained by his purpose and his goal.

He it was, with the advance guard, that came on a plantation which was apparently as deserted and clean-swept as any they had hitherto encountered on the march, but when the doors of a great barn were beaten open, out flooded a yellow tide of corn dried and glistening on the cob. Food for an army!

Those nearer the door acted in strange ways. Some of them, ordered by Kildare, with a mouth full of food obediently started to pitch the cobs out to a distance so that the rest of the running army could get to it.

Others fell down and began to cram their throats with the dry stuff until one of them choked and died on the spot. And Kildare saw one starved wretch on his knees, throwing up the corn, bathing his body in the joy of it, as it were, and blubbering and laughing with delight.

But they were saved. They had enough to eat and quantities to carry away. For the first time the city of Panama had reason to be concerned with this strange march of ragamuffins across the Isthmus on an impossible quest.

19

PANAMA AT LAST!

BEYOND THAT BARN which was their salvation, they encountered an Indian ambuscade—but without Indians inside it. The red men were on the farther side of the river, dancing and yelling and brandishing their bows and arrows in intervals of the trees.

A score of buccaneers plunged in at once to get across the river and capture a few of the Indians for what information might be tormented out of them, but five men were shot until they bristled with arrows, and their dead bodies floated down the stream into the mouths of the alligators, while the triumphant Indians started yelling in Spanish: *"Hai,* dogs! *Hai!* Go out on the savannah! Go out on the savannah! See what waits for you there!"

What waited there, the buccaneers wondered? A mighty armed force of the Spaniards ready to sweep the Morgan-men to death?

It was now time to prepare. They rested at the end of the sixth day; slept as well as they could with their bellies complaining of the quantities of dried corn which had been chewed down, and with fifty great fires smoking in the woods to keep away the damnation of the mosquitoes.

On the seventh day they furbished their swords, cleaned

the firearms, looked to the dryness of the powder, and then crossed the river and advanced until they saw before them one of the fairest sights that ever had blessed the eyes of a starving pirate—a whole trim little town with smoke rising from it. And why should there be fire in such a torrid climate unless cookery was going on?

Alas, as they ran into the town on the double, they discovered that the place had been swept clear of all provisions, and the smoke rose from the burning houses, for the Spaniards had fired the entire village, except the stone store-houses and stables of the King of Spain.

After heavenly expectation, nothing came to their stomachs except some starving dogs and cats in the streets, which were instantly butchered and devoured.

It was from this place that Morgan sent the boats down stream to rejoin those which waited under guard at Cedro Bueno; only one periagua he retained and hid to act as a messenger boat later on, in time of need. At the town of Venta Cruz, also, a party wandering for provisions outside of the town was surprised by a number of Spaniards and Indians, and one of the buccaneers captured and carried off. He would be tortured until he gave information; then he would be tortured again until he died. Perhaps the generous Spaniards would hand him over to the Indians, so that they might indulge themselves in the giving of the last rites of agony.

On the eighth day they found a road from Venta Cruz and took it, many of the men still very sick but able to walk. The road was rough with cobblestones, but to men used to wearying their arms at the oars or to struggling through forest slush the road was a heavenly delight. Here occurred a very strange thing, for brutes as they were, the buccaneers, not one of them stepped into or crushed a stream of green leaf-bits which was flowing out of the forest on one side, across the road, and into the forest on the other side. These were an army of the leaf-cutting ants which, said Luis the Mosquito, bury the leaves under the ground for the sake of the fungus which will grow on them, and on which they afterwards feed. That green, living stream, each ant carrying a portion of leaf far larger than his own body, flowed uninterrupted straight across the path of the marching men, as though even the buccaneers could sympathize with labors which were greater than their own!

Indians now began to shoot arrows at them from covert but only a few men were slightly wounded. Finally the redmen gained the courage to stand their ground in a covert of trees, rallying strongly about a cacique. But this was easy game for the buccaneers. They charged with a wild joy, glad to have for the first time a chance to get their hands on human enemies. They burst in among the redmen, killed the chief, and scattered the rest like smoke.

AND NOW, STILL going downhill towards the South Sea, they left the forest and had before them a pleasant country, green, checkered with farms, and in a little valley between two ridges of hills they camped for the night. It was a wretched encampment, with a dark smother of rain constantly falling, but not a man murmured. The prize they had come for so far was not long removed from them now!

And on the morning of the ninth day they marched in a mass across the next ridge and there saw before them a landscape worthy of heaven, they thought.

And at the foot of the hills appeared some Spanish

cavalry with morions and breastplates on fire in the slant morning light. They scattered and rode off slowly, firing a few vain, distant shots from their heavy carbines.

Beyond, lay the open, green savannah where the Indians had assured them they would find something worth seeing. But beyond the green plain lay the cloudy smoke of the town of Panama, beyond that the deep blue of the Pacific, and in the sea—how tiny it seemed in the distance!—a tall ship under a white cloud of sail.

And southward lay the Andes, clearly seen, whitening their tops in the sky, like spear-heads gilded with silver light. And on the plain below them—better than all the beauty which greeted the spirit and the eye, they saw a scattering of grazing cattle!

They were rounded up, butchered; fires smoked, burned, were almost put out under the mass of raw flesh which the pirates approached to the flames. Men were seen with blood dripping down their faces, spilling on their clothes as they tore with savage teeth at half-roasted pieces of beef.

Corn? That had been horse food, but this was the food for men! They feasted; they rested; they feasted again; and then got up after a long noonday rest and went staggering forward, laughing, drunk with content, forgetful of all the danger and the gain that might lie before them, rather thinking back to the banquet on roasted flesh as the greatest moment of their lives.

So it was late in the day, almost the end of it, when a thin, dark spearhead grew up out of the savannah in front of Kildare and the vanguard. His eyes could not discern its nature, at first, but after a moment he understood. It was the first, the tallest spire of Panama.

They topped the next rolling piece of ground and saw before them all the wide walls, the lights of Panama beginning to gleam through the twilight.

There was no riot of joy. The men laughed, and clapped one another on the shoulder. A thousand such proud cities turned to spoil, a mule load of gold for every man in the army, would have seemed unimportant compared with that last meal of roasted flesh which was inside them, already sending strength into their bodies and a sort of foggy joy into their brains.

20

KILDARE'S PLANS

BEFORE THE SUN had set on this day, Kildare was talking with Henry Morgan, whom he found in very good spirits now that the forthcoming decisive battle was not far off.

Morgan said, merely: "Their scouts tell them that we're half starved, ragged, weak, exhausted. They're going to come out with every man from the town who's equipped with guns and they're going to try to sweep us off the field at a charge. If we beat them, Tranquillo, we'll run with them all the way inside Panama; and beat them we shall because we have to. In the meantime, if you have a hundred men, get them and bring them to me."

"When you show yourself on the field to-morrow," said Kildare, "suppose that armed ship sailed into Panama harbor and made an attack? How many of the Spaniards opposite you would be unsteadied if they heard guns and yells and alarm bells beating from the harbor side of the town?"

Here Jimmy Green, the ape, found something on the ragged sleeve of Kildare that attracted his attention. He shambled over on all fours and reached out his black paw. Kildare took the paw in his hand. "Jimmy Green congratulates me on the idea," said Kildare.

At this Morgan laughed. "You have the brain for an admiral," he declared. "Where will you find your ship?"

"They will come back continually, I think, to a certain lagoon that I know of down the coast below the city."

"Why will they make that their harbor if the Spaniards might trace them to the place—aye, and perhaps capture them because they keep coming back to the same place like rabbits to a warren?"

"I left them there," said Kildare. "They will keep hoping to find me there again."

Morgan hesitated. "Well," he said, "if I let you go, I think that I'm giving up a part of my good luck. But go to try your chance."

"There were three horses, saddled and all, captured to-day on the savannah," said Kildare.

"We won't eat them while we have beef," said Morgan.

"Give me two of them, one for myself and one for Luis."

Morgan scowled. He was not a man to give anything away easily. But eventually he shrugged his shoulders. "Take the horses and go your way, Tranquillo," he said. He scratched the tuft of whiskers between his lower lip and chin. Jimmy Green hopped up and sat on his master's shoulder and made odd faces at the Englishman. "Go, and take your luck with you," continued Morgan. "I think that I'll see you in Panama before many days—maybe we'll meet over brandy; maybe we'll meet in a Spanish torture chamber."

Far through the night rode Kildare and Luis, the Mosquito Indian, until Luis was riding first on one leg and then on the next, because a great deal of his skin had been chafed away. He made no complaint, however, as they struck from the savannah into woods, and from the woods came out by the waters of a lagoon where clear moonlight turned the sea to black and silver.

And there—not drawn up on the beach but moored with light cables in the shallow of the water, its bows pointing out to the bay, lay the good galley, the Santa Magdalena. Two or three fires smoked faintly along the beach with forms lying asleep near them—always on the lee side of the fires, so that the smudge might keep the mosquitoes off. But what pleased Kildare on seeing the Santa Magdalena, almost unbelievably returned to that trysting place, what pleased him almost as much as seeing the ship and the crew was the sight of dark forms walking on sentry go along the beach and in the ship itself. That would be the contriving of Louis d'Or, of course.

A moment later there was a loud shout and a musket exploded, the bullet singing a harsh high note not far from the head of Kildare himself.

The whole camp sprang up, with a glimmering bit of steel in the hand of every man. Even as Kildare shouted to identify himself, he could see some of the big, dusky forms of the negroes nearest at hand with their arms drawn back at full strain and their longheaded spears ready for the cast.

Five seconds later he was gripping the hands of Padraic More and the Frenchman. The fires were lighted. Meat began to hiss on the flames. Meat of many kinds—of waree, and agouti, and fresh pork, and venison. Cocoa was brewing, bread was being broken, wine and brandy produced, cases of bottles of delicate liquors gleamed in fire-shine and moonlight, and a wide, wild voice of rejoicing went ringing up from the beach and echoing across the flat silver waters of the lagoon.

KILDARE STOPPED THAT outcry and that festival with brief words.

"All my friends," he said, "we can't drink to-night and fight to-morrow, and to-morrow morning we are going to sail into Panama harbor and attack the forts."

"We?" said Captain Bartholomew, lisping with his toothless gums. "We attack the forts of Panama—and then we tackle her thirty thousand people, I suppose?"

But Louis d'Or said: "Morgan has come, I suppose? Is that it, Tranquillo? We've had some word about him from the last two or three little boats we captured coming out of Panama!"

Kildare looked at his friends, and then over the sleek ribs of the negroes, who grinned and nodded whenever they felt his eyes on them. Suddenly he felt like a starved cat. "You've had a fat time of it," he said.

"Never a day without rowing," said Louis d'Or, with a smile. "And sometimes hardly a day without a prize of one sort or another. The Spaniards have come to know us, Tranquillo. They've hunted the seas for us with whole flotillas; but the weather has been good. In a fair wind we sail away from them; in a calm, we row away. We've led charmed lives—but so have you, or you would never have managed to lead Henry Morgan by the nose across the Isthmus of Darien for the sake of setting your lady free. What did you do to manage that?"

"Told some truth and a good many lies," said Kildare. "And Morgan is waiting with a thousand men on the savannah outside of Panama. They'll fight the battle to-morrow."

"A thousand men? Tranquillo, the Spaniards will eat them! They have Indians enough, alone, to fill the air with arrows and spit every one of Morgan's men ten times over!"

"Perhaps. But not one of Morgan's men will die without making a fight of it. And suppose, in the middle of the fight in the savannah, that guns are heard in the harbor, and the alarm begins to go yelling up from the town?—Every fighting man among the Spaniards has a family or a bit of treasure in the town. They'll begin to look over their shoulders before long—and trust Morgan then to make them run, aye, and to come tumbling into the town at their heels! You've lived on the fat, Louis d'Or. Now we'll do a little fighting, and afterwards you can go home and buy the king's peace in France as you please. Mark—when we sail into the harbor we'll find that it's been stripped of every soldier to fight on the landward side. Think of the booty there along the quay?"

THAT THOUGHT WAS enough to end all argument; and not half an hour later the drinking had ended, the negroes were stretched murmuring together around the fires, Kildare had finished in a very brief sketch the account of his adventures, and now as he stretched himself out in his turn on the sand, Luis the Indian came and squatted for a moment at his side.

"There are more than a hundred of them gathered here, father," he said.

"Aye, more than a hundred," murmured Kildare, sleepily.

"And ten of your hundreds more waiting on the savannah to fight to-morrow."

"That is true."

"And all of this," said Luis the Indian, "is because one man wants one woman."

"I can't tell, Luis. It's a hunger they give us; like the hunger for sun when the sky is raining, and the hunger for shade when the sun is burning."

"True," said Luis. "Then there must be a devil in a woman."

21

UNDER FIRE

IN THE DAWN of the next morning, there was hardly enough wind to wipe the oily look from the face of the sea. And with furled sails and the long yards pointing fore and aft, the Santa Magdalena sped out to sea and sent the water singing down her long sides. She went with a will.

Those gaunt, round-backed negroes of the other days had been able to make the galley jump through the waves with the whip to inspire them, but the full flowing muscles and the happy spirits of these re-made oarsmen gave them a doubled power.

They sang as they worked, always one voice chanting a time for the others to follow, while Padraic More sat under the awning and laughed and beat out the rhythm with the gavel, and the great, red mouths of the negroes grinned back at him.

The foul odor had left the ship—unless it were for a slightly sour smell such as comes from wood that has been impregnated with wine. And the entire air of the very galley itself seemed to have altered. The rigging was more trim and taut, kept as it was by the skilful direction of that hardy seaman, Bartholomew.

There was no cluttering of marines. The English were

the sailors assisted by a few picked negroes. But the negroes themselves were the marines, and very proud of them was Captain Louis d'Or as he stood on the poop and explained to Kildare what had been done.

Louis d'Or was in truth a figure of gold, now, for he had found in one prize a splendid suit of yellow velvet, complete from hat to shoes, and he shone like metal in the sun, with his hair a brighter sheen than the silk of the cloth.

From the first they had had plenty of muskets and carbines. And from the prizes they made they had taken more until every oarsman in the galley had a good gun under his bench, together with at least a pair of those terrible spears with cutlasses for lance-heads. And each negro was girt with a belt from which swung an excellent machete.

Having the weapons was only a small part of the game, and Louis d'Or, the Irishman, and Bartholomew had encouraged the negroes constantly to practice with the muskets. For that matter, they had more powder and lead than they could use, and the result of establishing a few prizes and distributing a bit of instruction and praise was that every one of the blacks had become a tolerable marks-man; some were truly excellent, though none of them had quite that deadly perfection which the buccaneers were apt to possess.

However, they had taken over a hundred desperate slaves and turned them into five score cheerful, reckless fighting men. Though in a pinch, said Louis d'Or, the negroes were apt to trust more to the lances than to the muskets.

"And perhaps they ought to," said the Frenchman, "for

I've seen them stand off ten paces and then drive the head of the spear through an inch plank!"

So they were talking, very gaily, as though they had not decided to run straight into the lion's mouth on this day. They raised the smoke of Panama town; they saw the gleam of the highest steeple, and now, well out to sea, they saw a huge ship under a great white head of sail.

Louis d'Or turned instantly towards it. There was no need to guess what was in it. Such a ship of such a size would not have left Panama on an idle errand, and they could be sure that half the treasure of the city had been packed on board before it left the quay.

In the slight wind they saw the great boat turning slowly to cover them with its broadside.

And what a broadside! Through the open ports looked the huge, ring-mouthed and reënforced muzzles of twenty-five great guns!

"She's the Santo Spirito!" cried the Irishman, though he kept the rhythm duly with his gavel. "See the blacks laugh! God knows they'd wear other faces if they knew what's on that ship! Four hundred Spaniards or my name is not More! Four hundred of the king's men, and seven hundred tons, and sixty guns—and—"

"Drake would have done the trick with three pinnaces and a hundred men on board, with nothing better than muskets to pick off the helmsmen and the gunners," said Kildare. "Why can't we do the same trick with a racehorse like this under us and some big guns of our own to do a little barking and biting? Bring up under her starboard quarter, Louis d'Or! The wind fails her and she sits still like a duck in thick mud. She can't yaw as fast as we can shift!"

THE GREAT SANTO Spirito, in fact, was now fixed in place, with the sails hanging in folds like the cheeks of old women, as the lithe, swift-running galley was maneuvering in a wide arc to come up behind her. Those heavy guns would be of little use unless trained directly on the enemy, and if the galley came in just angling from the corner of the stern, it would be hard for a single broadside gun to strike at her, and even the five huge stern-chasers would find it hard to strike their mark.

Right on this correct angle, Louis d'Or steered the galley. As they came up, they could see a frenzy of preparation on the Spaniard. He was big enough to laugh at such an antagonist, but not in such a deadness of the air that he could not maneuver. Into his five big fighting tops, high on the masts and at the end of the reaching bowsprit, he sent a crowd of men. On the decks, the crew were bringing aft some of the lighter deck guns. But it was no part of the purpose of the Santa Magdalena to venture up in close range. She would steal close and try to do what damage she could before a gust of wind enabled the monster to swing about and, with a single broadside, blow the frail galley from the face of the sea.

Stern-chasers, all five of them, roared from the Santo Spirito. The heavy shot plunged into the sea on the lee of the galley. The rearmost starboard guns of the Spaniard bellowed smoke and lead; but these shots went well to the right of the galley.

Even the negroes understood the meaning of this and set up a frantic yelling of delight. They could understand that they had stolen up exactly into the blind spot of the eye of the great ship.

The Spanish crew knew the same thing and a long howling of dismay came rolling over the water. There followed a great discharge of musketry and a barking of deck guns that curtained the lofty stern of the ship in white fog, and as this drifted very gradually away, the gilded carvings which ran and writhed from the water line to the top of the poop were, visible again.

"Now!" said Kildare. "Now let him have it. The stern first, Bartholomew! Knock out that eye of him entirely and we'll have a blind spot to dodge into and stay in if the wind brings him a bit of life!"

Bartholomew, a famous gunner, handled the aiming of the galley's largest gun; the two others, pointing forward, were aimed by the Irishman and Louis d'Or. They began a steady fire.

To Louis d'Or was assigned the task of hitting the mizzen mast and bringing it down if possible, because a ship without its rearmost mast answers the helm very clumsily. The Irishman, with Bartholomew, kept plunging shot into the towering gun galleries at the stern of the Spaniard.

A few rounds steadied their aim. The length of the galley gave them a very steady shooting platform. The sea was still. And now every great shot was plunging into the stern of the Spaniard.

They dismounted three of the five great guns at once. Every shot knocked up a cloud of splinters and brought fresh shouts of dismay from the Santo Spirito's crew. The galley was fixed, for the moment, in a perfect safety, like a small hawk at a height above an eagle's head, able to pounce when it would.

The fourth stern-chaser of the Spaniard was knocked over, and at that moment, as though greeting the new wound received, the crew of the Spaniard began a tumultuous cheering. Kildare, looking over the side, saw the reason.

In the near distance, the southern sea was darkening, and the darkness ran rapidly towards them. A wind was coming. Already they were swinging the yards, the great, heavy, creaking yards of the Santo Spirito to catch, the breeze when it arrived.

Already the rudder was turning with the pull of its chains. The first weight of the wind would now turns the huge ship to the starboard and bring his whole starboard battery, gun by gun, to bear on the galley.—and a single shot, taking proper effect, might rip the galley open from end to end and sink it on the spot.

KILDARE RAN FORWARD into the smoke which rose in pungent clouds about the guns of the Santa Magdalena, He shouted at the ear of Bartholomew: "A wind coming. We're lost unless I can keep straight in the rear of the Santo Spirito. We're lost even if I put the galley there, unless you can manage to knock over the last of the stern-chasers!"

A streak of powder-black, greasy as paint, was struck diagonally across the face of Bartholomew and made him look like a ghost, and a hellish one. He waved a hand of understanding at Kildare and bent to the sighting of the gun again.

Kildare cried to Louis d'Or: "Center the mizzen-mast again, Louis. Bring her down—or God help us! The wind is coming."

"I've hit the damned mast," said the Frenchman. "I'll

hit it again—but it's like whittling with a small knife at a great tree!"

Kildare ran back to his place in the stern and through his cupped hands shouted the order. At once the oars were in motion. The blacks, serenely confident, were still laughing to one another; what would happen to their morale if some solid shot began to plunge among them?

In the meantime, he swerved the galley right in behind the Spaniard, and at the same time the wind filled the sails of the big ship with an audible succession of booming noises. It leaned. The hull shook.

The water quivered along the edge of the moving hull, and now she began to answer her head and swing gradually to the starboard in the midst of a frantic pandemonium of joy; every man on the Spaniard seemed to have ten tongues of brass at that moment.

The rearmost gun of the starboard broadside boomed. The big shot whirred visibly through the air and streaked just past the right-hand gunwale of the galley. Kildare turned the galley still more. If he could maneuver well enough he might still avoid the fatal danger of the whole broadside and there remained only the single great stern-chaser.

Here, suddenly, it spoke. Even before the sound dinted against the ears of Kildare, a crackling ruin swept through the larboard benches of the Santa Magdalena. The sweeps snapped off like straws, the benches were broken; a hideous spray of blood rose in a flying cloud and dashed into the face of Kildare.

Ten of the blacks were down; the rest were in a howling confusion as Kildare himself leaped down among the broken benches and seized the handle of an unbroken sweep.

"Give, way! Give way!" he roared.

And as he shouted, looking up he could see through the great porthole where the mouth of the stern-chaser issued, the Spaniards in a dancing and screaming joy.

Moreover, as the galley rowed in, it of necessity had come much closer to the big ship, and now the cloud of men in the fighting top of the mizzen mast opened with a rapid musketry.

Here was the test of fire for the black men. Kildare, with a dizzy sense that he and all the rest were wavering on the sharp edge of destruction, was amazed to hear the shouting of the blacks turn from dismay to rage.

They leaped at the remaining sweeps on the port side. They stood on the mangled bodies of their kindred and strained at the oars as though they were striving to break them. But further ruin came.

THAT MOMENT OF delay had allowed the yawing Spaniard to swing still further around, and that rearmost pair of guns on the starboard battery spoke again. One shot fairly missed. The other snapped off the galley's mast and flung it with its confusion of rigging over the side.

Could they drag that weight forward and creep into the comparative safety of the stern of the Santo Spirito?

Slowly they pushed through the water, and rapidly the great ship was gathering way, swinging, coming to life like a sleeping lion to strike away a rabble of mongrel dogs.

Bartholomew, stripped to the waist, powder-blackened, would have to tell a part of the tale. He told his half that instant, for the round shot from his big gun smashed full into the muzzle of the last of the five stern-chasers. That great-mouthed token of ruin was flung from its carriage and the laughing, dancing gun-crew disappeared in the interior darkness. At the same moment the pressure of the wind leaned like a shoulder of a giant against the wounded mizzen mast of the Santo Spirito and brought it down with a long, rending crash. The men in the fighting top, like a handful of small shot, were flung afar into the sea.

22

RETREAT

FAR OUTSIDE PANAMA on the green savannah the Spaniards were maintaining their battle furiously but not very well. They had plenty of men and plenty of guns and if they could have fought hand-to-hand, the buccaneers could not have endured those numbers very long. But getting to close quarters was the difficulty. The cavalry kept up their charging until nearly all of them were dropped dead on the savannah, and they included most of the blue-blooded gentry of the city. Now crowds of the riderless horses were roving about the plain, caught by the buccaneers whenever possible so that the pursuit might be keen or retreat made easy if the time came for it.

The cavalry being beaten down at a distance, the Spanish foot found an equal trouble in getting forward, because holes appeared in their long line from the terrible, unfailing musket fire of the pirates, and as soon as one hole was closed, another appeared.

The Spanish governor had one last resort which he now applied. He had been a sick man for many days, and during the long, wakeful nights since he had known that the buccaneers were crossing the isthmus of Darien, he had evolved a brilliancy that could be murderously effective in the time of battle.

There were great droves of cattle scattered over the savannah and by degrees the governor had brought them up closer and closer to the city of Panama, so that the bellowing kept the air slightly atremble in Panama day and night, like a murmuring of distant thunder. As the battle began, these herds were driven in from east and west, the bulls crowded towards the front, the cows and calves to the rear, two huge, dark-fronted armies with the long, polished horns shining like weapons, like hordes of brandished swords. A throng of quick-footed Indians and negroes maneuvered the herds, pushing them forward, and at last getting them into a dead run. The two wings came thundering in on the flanks of the buccaneers while the Spanish line, which seemed in danger of being involved in the same dilemma, hastily drew back a little and began to shout with a sudden enthusiasm in this unlucky battle.

Admiral Henry Morgan proved himself more than a common pirate then. Everywhere, he could see his men wincing from what looked like certain death. A good number of them had already mounted the captured horses, and in a moment they would be apt to try to save their lives by flight.

The battle hung on a thread; but Morgan, turning his voice to a harsh thunder that was heard up and down the line, bade the flanks form facing outwards to meet the droves and then to hold fire until the herds were at a short distance. He himself would give the order to fire. And he ran off into the men of the left flank to take his stand on the site of the most dangerous ground.

*"Catch them and
burn them!"*

It was hard to persuade his men to hold their fire. They
were apt to use their guns when, and where they pleased,
once a fight had begun, and they could hear their fellows
on the right flank already opening, in spite of the orders
which Morgan had given.

But here Henry Morgan in person raged up and down,
sword in hand, with the white-bearded ape, Jimmy Green,
perched on his shoulder. The sight of Jimmy Green squeal-
ing and dancing on the shoulder of his master while bullets
were flying all around had had a wonderful effect in steady-
ing the nerves of the buccaneers, and now they obediently
held their fire.

The black-fronted herd of bulls rushed on very close
until the leaders had dropped their heads and begun the
final charge, as though they expected the next moment to
have their horns in human flesh. Then Morgan gave the
word with a great shout which the beating and the clashing
of the myriad hoofs could only partially drown. The whole

front of the flanking line burst into flashes of fire, and a simultaneous roar as the volley was poured in.

The buccaneers, their muskets empty, began to dance and screech and wave their arms and brandish their swords. In the meantime, the whole front of the charging herd went down, the ranks immediately behind tumbling head-long over the killed leaders. Those behind would sooner have charged into a raging fire than into the insane human tumult before them. Right and left the great herd split, like a stream of dark water on a rock, and roared harm-lessly away.

THAT WAS NOT all. From the right flank came yells of dismay. And Henry Morgan, looking back, saw that all his plans were about to be ruined; for though the scatter-ing fire of the buccaneers on that side had killed many of the beeves and turned others to the side, a considerable number broke through and rushed down the line.

Several of the pirates were trampled to death. The others along the line, thrown into a confusion, leaped here and there and fired for their lives.

It was a thinned herd that reached the center of the line and there bore down and ripped to tatters the English standard which Morgan had been careful to raise. But here, as though they had accomplished their purpose and real-ized that no more could be done, they turned and scattered harmlessly across the plain.

Much damage had been done, however. The entire buccaneer line was in confused disorder, weakened by the withdrawal of men to the flanking parties and, moreover, full of great gaps across the front.

The Spaniards were soldiers enough to see this. The

remaining handful of cavalry and all the infantry, pushed forward very gallantly, yelling out to the English: "Stand for us, dogs! Stand, Englishmen! We are going to send you to hell before your time! Santiago! Santiago! Forward, gentlemen."

They were charging home with these gallant outcries when through the air from the direction of Panama city came a sound of heavy booming, that made many a man look up suddenly to see thunderclouds.

But there were no thunderheads in the sky. The blue of it was washed and pure and every man in the Spanish host realized, suddenly and with a deadly coldness about the heart, that the noise was that of guns firing in the harbor.

There was a rear attack, then?

They could have guessed from the first that even a madman like the desperate Henry Morgan never would have delivered a frontal assault against an enemy so many times his strength except that he had ships to take the city from the rear.

The English, badly exhausted by the fighting, almost ready to run, marked that wavering among the Spaniards where every man had a family or a treasure to think of and who could not help picturing the rape and ruin of the city at his back.

Henry Morgan himself was the first to shout out, when he heard the guns: "Tranquillo! Tranquillo! He is in the city with five hundred men! The brave Tranquillo! He takes Panama behind your backs, while you wait out here like a lot of lazy dogs! Forward! Smash them, boys, before Tranquillo's hungry rats find all the good bits in the city.

Forward! Panama is ours! Tranquillo is eating the heart of the city now!"

The whole army, possessed by the same idea as the noise of the cannon became greater and greater, forgot their own danger and only were eager to get at the rich loot of the city. As the Spanish heart died at the sound of the cannon in the harbor, that of the buccaneers rose suddenly.

And they began to charge as the Spaniards were coming to an uncertain stand.

That ended the doubt about the battle. The buccaneers came in refreshed with confidence and forgetting their two hundred dead and all their wounds.

The Spaniards, divided between two ideas, could do nothing. At the first weight of the onset they gave way and crumbled in long, streaming lines towards Panama!

Henry Morgan followed. There were batteries to be taken and he had a mind to have them at once, entering on the heels of the Spaniards. Besides, there were many horses, now, to give wings to a big percentage of his host—horses, and mules which had been brought out as beasts of burden. Any back, any saddle would suit a buccaneer!

THE GALLEY WAS well behind the Spaniard, now, and this was indeed a blind spot and a broad one, for not a single gun other than a musket could now bear aft from the big ship. However, the battle was not over. The wind blew fresh. And the Santo Spirito had gathered such way that she had become very maneuverable, as the wreckage of the mizzen was cut away and allowed to drift free.

The wreckage of the foremast of the galley, on the other hand, was still clinging to her, though the machetes, keen as knives and heavy as axes, were working hard and fast to chop the cordage clean away.

And yonder was Louis d'Or, having done his duty so very well by the mizzen of the Spaniard, taking order about clearing of the wreck, while Bartholomew and the Irishman with a constant dint put one round shot after another through the stern ports of the Spaniard. Raking shots were all of these, which did not simply penetrate the ship from side to side, but ranged long fore and aft, caroming from one obstacle to dash into another.

Kildare saw the red spout out, boldly, from the scuppers of the stricken ship, or else run leaking down the tall sides of it. It was not battle on board her, for this moment, but sheer massacre. It was not imagining that made him see, time and again, the terrible red sheen of sprays of blood where the solid shot dashed whole groups of men to death.

But do as they would, still the clinging wreckage from the mast that was overboard held the galley crank and slow while the fair wind bowled the Spaniard along and turned him again to the starboard, he having by this time turned in such a circle that he was fairly pointed back again for Panama. And very much most of those aboard him must have wished to be ashore again!

Here, however, he had veered so that, one by one, every gun on the starboard broadside bore on the galley.

There was not a shot fired. Kildare felt that he understood. The wise captain, saving patiently his wrath and his pain, now had determined to hold his fire until all a broadside bore on the enemy and then, in one blood-red instant, to blow him to a fiery hell.

And still the volley did not come!

Only then was the wreckage of the galley's mast cleared away and the good light ship sped into the water again—to get that priceless advantage point astern of the galleon—with sweeping strokes of the oars, with Kildare shouting loudly to give the rhythm for the sway and catch of the sweeps.

And he realized, as the galley roused herself, what had happened. There was no fire from the starboard guns. There would be no fire from them for some moments.

The frightful storm of shot which had swept again and again the lower gundecks of the Spaniard had driven the guncrews up to the top deck and the guns, the great, fatal guns which looked with wide eyes on the pirate, were not served!

That was how Kildare ran his boat from under the verge of death and back, safely, without a cannon fired, under the stern of the Spaniard.

There were not even muskets playing, now, from the great ship, except from the two fighting tops of the mainmast, and Captain Bartholomew most wisely and sufficingly took care of these; for he loaded his great gun, which already had won the battle for the buccaneers, clean to the muzzle with musket balls, aimed it nicely, and sent such a cloud of death on the men in the fighting tops that half of them were gone in an instant, and the rest slid down stays or clambered down the shrouds to escape from another terrible visitation.

The battle, clearly, was now over. The voice of agony that rang unceasingly from the Spaniard told that the work had been done. It only needed that the galley should run aboard the galleon and probably the shock of a hand-to-hand attack would end the matter, no matter what odds of men still remained aboard the Santo Spirito.

However, another agency here was taking a blind hand, and that was the freshening wind. No longer striving to use it to maneuver so as to bring fresh broadsides to bear on the pirates, the Spaniards were running as fast as they could, with all sails spread on the fore and mainmasts, towards the shelter of Panama harbor.

Would that be a shelter, after all?

Far away, dim and small with distance but unmistakable, the sound of guns blew on the wind from the landward side of Panama. What was happening there?

IF THE SPANIARDS on the shore, hearing the guns of the sea-battle, shrank away, Morgan certainly would scatter them. But if the Spaniards used their numbers to win, then the galley was running in the jaws of death by entering the range of the forts of the bay.

This Louis d'Or—his golden clothes badly streaked and stained with fresh blood—came running aft to shout to Kildare. But Kildare, grinning till the smile pulled painfully at his face, answered: "We are running on a high tide. If it takes us to hell, what does that matter? Have you forgotten, Louis? Have you forgotten the treasure of Tranquillo, and the church of San Francisco?"

"No," said the Frenchman, "no more than you have forgotten that Spanish girl of yours."

"Brother," said Kildare, "she only wears a Spanish name. Her soul is like her complexion—English, all English!"

Then he added: "Make on! Close on them, friends! Forward before she reaches the dock. There is gold on her. Gold and silver. We are rich men!"

The negroes had cast their dead men overboard, and standing where their broken, red-stained benches cluttered the places, they sprang on the oars and made the prow of the galley rise with the force of their rowing.

So, rapidly, the galley closed on the Santo Spirito, but the wind was strong enough to speed the Spaniard into the bay and close up towards the quay. Now the English were within the range of the forts, yet no gun fired.

Kildare laughed: "They are all out there on the savannah! Every man of them has left the town to fight in the field! And what fighting! Do you hear, Louis d'Or?"

It was unmistakable.

Kildare and his friends were not able to see that picture of flight, but they could make out, very well, a thin, distant sound, no louder than the singing of one bird near at hand, and that sound was made up of human voices and rolled constantly closer and closer to the landward walls of Panama.

There was only one meaning for it. The Spaniards were in swift retreat, and if they retreated before such devils as those of Henry Morgan, they were lost! And Panama would be lost with them.

Perhaps the Spaniards on the Santo Spirito understood the distant noises and the far approach of gunfire in the same way. This, at least, is the truth. That when the great ship came close to the quay, the main course was thrown suddenly aback, and the ship checked her way and glided with a wonderful smoothness up towards the edge of the quay.

The moment she was near, men began to leap from the decks. Some fell short, struck the water, and were crushed to death as the rounded side of the galleon bumped against the quay. But the majority leaped safely to the quay and then fled with their lives, and no honor.

This was not true of all. There were always among the Spaniards of the New World a certain few who had not fallen entirely from the high estate of the old Castillian blood, men like those who made the greatest infantry in the world under the command of the great Parma and others, men whose blood had not been weakened by tropic weather and the gold hunger. And there were a certain number on board the Santo Spirito who had not the slightest intention of abandoning the great ship before she was sunk under them.

Among these was their calm commander, a hero, a gentleman, a pure soul of valor and gentleness who had wasted his own fortune instead of finding one, he was so apt to give gifts of medicine and food to the poor Indians he found.

This was Francisco Mores, now rather old, rather bent, but very young at heart and ever ready to die. Francisco Mores rallied all who would follow him and led them aft onto the high poop of the galleon where he prepared to beat off the attack of the pirates.

Poor Francisco Mores!

But how could he know that there would be on board the galley a subtle and ready serpent like Ivor Kildare, who would not even try, like most of his shipmates, to storm the lofty wall of the Santo Spirito but instead chose to slip with a few followers through the broken timbers, the batters, yawning portholes at the stern of the galleon, and so to make their way into the intimate vitals of the ship?

IT WAS A frightful journey, one made as though into an underworld. Dead men—and more dead fragments—were here and there to be stumbled over, and the big beams that crossed the decks above were spattered with brain and with blood, and most of the cannon of the starboard battery tumbled from their carriages and were now rolling with a soft thunder back and forth over the planks.

But Kildare led his men upwards from the lower decks. They reached a cabin where bottles of wine rolled on the floor, and where by some freak of chance a jewel casket was open on the table of the cabin, a great casket with little labels attached to rings, to necklaces, to great, green and red-glowing pendants. The negroes who followed Kildare as though he were their king paid no heed to this display of cold fire, Kildare himself picked up a handful of the treasures of the ladies of Panama which had been labelled and entrusted to the keeping of the brave Don Francisco. He dropped those brilliants into his pocket and then climbed to the top-deck.

There were a score of the negroes behind Kildare when he came to the top-deck. They did not have to be shown the enemy or ordered forward. They ran like hungry animals up the blood-dripping decks towards the Spaniards on the poop of the Santo Spirito. There the long-bladed spears did the work thoroughly, quickly. Every Spaniard went down; every Spaniard who went down died instantly; and the remaining tide from the galley now swept up and gained the deck of the galleon.

They knew the state of the ship at once. It was Bartholomew himself who came up in a frenzy of joy and announced that whole tons and masses of silver were stored in the hold. He wanted to sail the galleon instantly out of the harbor and make home with it around the Horn.

Louis d'Or said: "Stay here with the ship. Get the sails trimmed. More and Kildare and I have a little trip to make on shore. But get the ship away from the quay and ready to stand out to sea—because if Morgan's men find her, they'll have everything that's inside her skin in no time at all!"

To Bartholomew it seemed an unspeakable madness to venture into the town and mix with the men of Morgan whose wild yelling could be heard on the farther rim of the city as they entered on their conquest. Padraic More enforced the same point of view.

"Tranquillo, man," he implored, "we have a ship to sail in and plenty of the Dew of Heaven on board her. We're only a step from England, now; but once we go on shore we may be a million miles from home. It's harder to get past Henry Morgan than to wade across the Pacific and the Atlantic, laid end to end. And if he smells money on us, you'll see him turn into a mad dog!"

Louis d'Or said: "There's enough to make us all rich in the hold of the Santo Spirito. Give up the thinking about the jewels in the church of San Francisco. Give up the girl, Tranquillo, too! There are a thousand prettier ones in your own England. It's only the distance from home that's made her seem so lovely."

Kildare said, while his anxious eye flashed away towards the uproar which was streaming into Panama town: "Stay here with the ship, both of you. I'll manage some way to come out to you. Stand a little way out into the harbor, and I'll get off to you in a small boat. And if not—"

He waved to them and instantly was over the side and swinging down onto the quay.

He ran with all speed straight for the house of Larretta.

Stone below and timber above, it was finished to the roof, now, and had an air of substantial wealth and comfort about it.

The front door was not locked and Kildare flung it open, shouting the name of Ines Heredia.

After the blazing brightness of the street, the house had the cool, dark loneliness of twilight, and the echoes of Kildare's shouting rang emptily back to him.

He reached her room. It was empty. A long red cloak trailed from the floor to the couch. It seemed to the frantic mind of Kildare like a living thing or a ghost of life flung down in a despairing posture; then he raced down the stairs. There he found a poor wretch of a servant of the house. He could hardly speak.

THE SAVAGE ENGLISHMAN caught the servant by the shoulder. He needed the prick of the stiletto point against the bone of his forehead before he stammered out that his mistress was with another woman at the Church of San Francisco.

Kildare left the house on the run. As he sped down the street he saw a dust cloud billowing not far from him, and out of the mouth of a lane rushed a burst of Spanish fugitives from the battlefield.

They had thrown away all weapons to lighten their flight and still they were not far ahead of the pursuit, for now Kildare saw three ragged men waving machetes and yelling triumph as they galloped on a trio of mules. The Spaniards themselves seemed hardly less dangerous to Kildare than these recent companions of his.

The church doors yawned wide open and he thought, as he leaped through them, that an organ was playing a strange lament. It was only the moaning of many voices. And now as his eyes grew accustomed to the dull light of the interior, he could see them on their knees before the high altar and at the shrines. And some lay on their faces with outstretched arms praying, weeping.

He called the name of Ines Heredia. The sound of his voice rolled slowly back to him on a faint and minor key. But not a one of the figures stirred.

He was in despair, bewildered, when two men ran into the church behind him. They were Louis d'Or and Padraic More, and they laid stern hands on him.

The Frenchman panted: "We could not let you go, Tranquillo. But Morgan's men have come as far as the quay. The Santo Spirito can't delay much longer or the devils will be at her in small boats and swallow her at a gulp. Tranquillo, let everything go and come with us! Damn the treasure in San Francisco's church."

"I'd rather give up the eyes out of my head," said Kildare. "She's here in this church. I'm thinking nothing of the treasure. Help me find her, brothers!"

"Shall we carry him away by force?" demanded Padraic More.

"We'd have to kill him first," said Louis d'Or. "This damned English stubbornness!—Have you searched in the crypt, Tranquillo?"

They found the way to it at once, and cowering in corners

of the lower room, shrinking away under the cobwebbed arches of the vaulting, they found a score of women.

"Ines!" cried Kildare.

She came to him suddenly out of the heart of a small group in a corner. There was not much light to see her by, but the Irishman exclaimed: *"Hai,* Tranquillo! No wonder you brought Morgan to Panama for this. I had forgotten, for one."

Louis d'Or said nothing at all. But he took off the plumed and sword-slashed and red-streaked tatters of his yellow velvet hat as he stared at the girl.

There was no time for a greeting; there was only a moment for Kildare to hold her away from him by the arms and reassure his eyes that they had not lied to his imagination all these days of the separation.

"Louis d'Or," said Kildare, "can we take her through the streets like this? We could never get from Panama to the ship with a woman like Ines."

"We can try," said Louis d'Or, still staring in a queer, helpless way at the girl. For he was seeing her not as on that day when he parted her and Kildare and let her drift back into the hands of the Spaniards, but as by revelation in the dim light of the crypt he watched her face and saw the tremor that shook Kildare.

"We can try," said Louis d'Or. "There are three of us, and we can keep her in the center. Are you ready, Tranquillo?"

Here the voice of the Irishman broke in on them.

He was pointing his huge hand toward the wall, where many a grave, in long rows, was stepped by stones, on some of which were mere inscriptions, and on others carved coats-of-arms. It was at one of these that Padraic More pointed, and went stalking toward it like a man entranced.

"The peacock!" he cried. "By God, the peacock of Tranquillo!"

It might have been intended as a bird with spread wings, for the carving was curiously rude and childish, but certainly the imagination could make the image into that of a peacock.

"Behind the peacock's tail—" said Louis d'Or.

He took the broad blade of his dagger and stabbed it repeatedly into the crevices around the stone to loosen the mortar, but in fact the stone was very slightly held. At the third or fourth stroke it slipped and then fell out like a hinged door.

The big fist of Padraic More was instantly in the aperture that opened, and he jerked out a little sack of brown leather, opened and poured into the great cup of his palm a stream of crimson and red and crystal white fires.

They soaked up all the light in the dim crypt; they blinded two of those adventurers with delight.

All the gold and the silver that weighted the huge hull of the Santo Spirito was as nothing compared to this burning Dew of Heaven!

23

SAMKIN'S DEATH

THEY HURRIED INES Heredia into the upper church and found it a different world. More women were packed into it, and a long, endless tremor of mournful sound kept passing and repassing through the nave.

Outside, other noises sounded—the loud, cracking explosion of a pistol, the shouting of men who had opened their throats and their hearts and grown drunk with the wine of victory.

Kildare, in the shadowy door of the church, waited for a moment and could not give the word to issue into the street. A weakness came over him, a sickness of heart that made him want to shrink back with the girl into a corner of the church like those suppliant women.

"On with you," urged the Irishman.

"Wait," said Louis d'Or, "It's no easy way that's before them now. Cover your face with that veil, *señorita*. For if they see you—"

Kildare, with his own hand, drew the veil across her face. She kept on smiling and saying that she was not afraid, but the moment that the veil was over her features, it seemed to him that she was already dead, and a dim ghost.

Then he mustered his courage and they went out onto the street.

To the Indian he said: "Stay close! You shall have your half of my loot, Luis."

The Indian only laughed.

"Father," he said, "what can I have more than a boat, a spear, and irons for striking the turtles?"

They came out of the dimness of the church into the bright glare of the open day and found in the air the wild uproar of the stricken town and the victors.

There was a queer, heady pungency of perfume which came from a place just down the street where a good number of the buccaneers, letting more precious loot go, were rolling brandy kegs out of a warehouse and knocking in the heads of them.

And wherever they looked they saw houses being broken open, or heard inside the houses the splintering of wood as doors were battered down, and always the continual screaming, pitched so high from the purest terror that it was often impossible to tell whether men or women were crying out.

There was the third element to make the horror perfect. Smoke was sweeping over the town in increasing volume every moment; the retreating Spanish governor had fired the town in a dozen places, and the rising wind was carrying the flames swiftly forward.

That could be forgotten if only they could get to the Santo Spirito and begin to lengthen out blue leagues of sea between them and the condemned city. Swiftly they hurried.

Hunchbacked Samkin, a pirate, staggered out of a house

under a great load of goods, cast it down and shouted loudly a greeting to Kildare.

"Well done, Tranquillo! When they heard you knocking at the door they all ran home and let us in the back way. Ha! ha! ha! Oh, Tranquillo, well done!"

Kildare, waving his hand, would have passed on, but Samkin had seen something in the step and the clothes of Ines Heredia, and his long arm reached out like that of an ape and snatched the veil from the brightness of her hair and face. The spear of Luis, the Indian, was instantly in the throat of Samkin. He could not even cry out, but fell on his face and kicked at the dust while the blood gushed out in a red pool.

"Murder! *Hai!* Murder!" shouted a dozen voices of buccaneers all in a moment, "They've killed Samkin."

AND A BIG black-faced man with beard almost to the eyes roared out: "Samkin, are you dead? By God, I'll have a payment for you! Tranquillo, give me the Indian dog!"

"Ay, give us the Indian!" shouted the gathering crowd.

And they came running, bent on trouble.

"You have to give him up," said Louis d'Or softly, at the ear of Kildare. "There's no other way—or the girl will be in danger along with the rest of us."

"Give him up?" said Kildare. He stared at the Indian. "I'll give up my own soul first. *Hai*, brothers! Samkin has a value and I'll pay you for him. You there, with the beard. I'll pay you down a good value for Samkin—but he was drunk, and he stumbled onto the point of the Indian's spear."

"You can pay cash afterwards. I'll have the damned redskin first," said the big buccaneer. He was one of the

few who carried a long cut-and-thrust rapier instead of a
handy machete, and he had the weapon out at once.

But he did not rush in on Kildare. The reputation of that
swordsman was too great for his fame to be clouded even
by the brandy which had obscured the brain of the buccaneer. He stood with his long blade ready and sang out to
his companions: "There's Tranquillo with a girl under his
arm that will ransom for a thousand pounds if ever I saw
woman. And now he's laid my brother Samkin dead and
won't pay us the Indian that did it. Is that justice? Tranquillo and that damned fop of a Frenchman, Louis d'Or,
that cut the throat of Captain Ogden at Port Royal—and
More, the Irishman—are the three of them to put down
the free gentlemen of the sea?"

It was not much of a speech, but it rang like bells in the
ears of the gathering company of buccaneers.

"Justice for the Brothers of the Coast!" they began to
shout, "Give up the Indian, Tranquillo."

"Now it's that or dying," said Louis d'Or.

Kildare looked wildly around him and saw that they
were just in front of the door of a house.

He said to More: "We can't keep ourselves in the open
street, God help us! But we can hold them from behind
that door. Pistol the lock of it and we'll get through."

"Ay, and never come out again," growled More.

"Then go on, the pair of you!" exclaimed Kildare. "Take
Ines on to the boat—but I can't leave Luis."

The Frenchman exclaimed: "There's no other way.
Quickly—with us, *señorita!* Tranquillo will come on at
once—"

"*Hai*, Blackbeard!" shouted one of the buccaneers.

"Samkin is as dead as stinking fish. What shall we do about it?"

It was true that the huge hands of Samkin no longer kneaded the red mud of the street. He lay still and wallowed no more.

"I'll have blood for him!" yelled Blackbeard. "Who's with me to tackle that dancing devil of a Tranquillo? Who's a friend at my shoulder?"

There was a general chorus of agreement. The rules of the Brotherhood were both strict and definite. A fair duel was nobody's business, but murder found an instant punishment as Morgan himself had learned with bitter cost, on a time when half his host had left him.

And here the girl, slipping from the protecting arm of tall Louis d'Or, ran back to Kildare.

The Frenchman himself brought out his sword, now, with a sweep that made several of the closing semicircle of buccaneers give ground.

"The door, Pat!" he called to More. "There's nothing for it but this!"

The pistol of More that moment exploded, and his foot kicked in the front door of the house.

"Charge them!" cried Blackbeard. "Do you see they're opening a line of retreat? Charge 'em home!"

The charge came, big capable men with reaching machetes closing on the defenders.

THE SWINGING BLADE of Louis d'Or nicked the head of one and staggered him so that he fell across the path of others and set them stumbling and falling. Before the charge had gathered head again, the small party had run through the door of the Spanish house into a momentary

safety at least. The long blade of Louis kept back an eager
trio of buccaneers until the door could be slammed and
furniture dragged to pile against it.

Pistol bullets were smashing through the woodwork by
this time. But a party of buccaneers were not apt to be held
out of a house simply because the door was closed to them.
Some of them commenced to batter against the shutters
on both sides of the house, threatening to break in through
the windows at any time.

"The back way?" called Kildare anxiously.

Padraic More was already returning with a gloomy face
from the rear of the house.

"They've blocked us in on all sides," he said. "Damn the
hand and the head of that Indian for running his spear into
the throat of Samkin! They're going to cut up the whole
batch of us, now."

It was only a moment later, in fact, that two of the
shutters were beaten in, and after that the influx poured
through the lower floor of the house. The stairs offered the
only retreat, and the party poured up them; beneath, the
buccaneers closed in a shouting wave about the last way
of apparent escape.

24

FOUR EMERALDS

FOUR ARMED MEN made a force strong enough to guard the narrows of that stairway and even those headlong brutes at the bottom of the steps did not attempt to storm the narrow way. They shouted their threats. Some would have blown the house to bits with a charge of powder, but others pointed out that the fire which was sweeping Panama soon would drive the rats out of their safety.

The flames had increased rapidly before a rising wind. Volleys of sparks and swiftly rolling clouds of smoke washed about the upper windows on the landward side, and out the windows that overlooked the harbor they saw the streaming smoke pour on across the blue of the bay.

There was something else of a painful interest on the bay.

The Santo Spirito had been ordered to stand a bit out from land, but now she was actually under full sail, with the galley, Santa Catalina, urging after her as fast as oars could be strained through the water. The benches of the galley had been filled with Spaniards driven in by the captors.

Now they did the work of the slaves while a crowd of the armed buccaneers filled the places of marines. Once that mob came to handstrokes with Bartholomew and his crew of whites and blacks, the Santo Spirito was sure to change hands quickly.

And the galley was gaining with a startling speed on the big ship which should have furnished Kildare and the rest with the long bridge back to England. That bridge was gone, whether the Santo Spirito escaped now and continued on her way, or whether it were captured by Morgan's men.

The many oars beat at the water. The handling of them was clumsy enough, and Kildare could see the bright little flashes of water as the blade of a sweep struck clumsily into the waves. Still there was sufficient manpower to make the galley run up on the great ship.

The Santo Spirito at last could no longer trust to her heels. The galley had opened fire. White puff after puff rose from her bows and the hollow booming sound drifted back to the ears of Kildare and his silent party. Those round shot could not be doing the crew of the Santo Spirito any good. And at any moment one of the two remaining masts might be knocked over.

That was why the galleon luffed. One by one the big bright muzzles of the port broadside gleamed on the eye. But the whole broadside was bearing before a single gun spoke. After that came a great puff of white that obscured the Santo Spirito from the sea-level to the topmasts.

What was happening behind that cloud of white was hard to tell, but the damage done to the galley was very visible. Kildare could see splinters of gunwale and oars leap up like dust. The rowers, thrown into helpless disorder, allowed their boat to drift helplessly, and then the buccaneers could be seen springing down to the oars.

It was as Kildare saw this that he heard the crashing roar of the broadside come with an echo over the sea. The Santa Catalina was being turned by Morgan's men and driven at full speed away from the peril of a second volley as terrible as the first.

At this a great shouting of rage went up from a great number of the buccaneers, who were gathered along the quay; and Kildare saw the white-bearded face of Jimmy Green above the heads of the rest, raised as he was on the shoulder of his master.

Morgan himself was brandishing a cutlass in a furious rage; no doubt he knew that half the treasure in his conquered city was now weighting down the hold of a ship that would never be his. He left the quay, and Kildare, before the intervening roofs shut him from view, could see the master pirate mounting one of a herd of the Spanish cavalry horses which stood about the quay.

That way to England was closed—that long way around the Horn. What remained to Kildare and the girl, at the best, even if they managed to escape from the trap which held them, except to struggle overland across the isthmus and then vaguely wander in the hope of finding return passage on some trading vessel?

But that future was so dim and dangerous that Kildare dared not look forward to it.

HE LOOKED DOWN at the girl and found that her eyes were fixed on him constantly. The moment that she felt his glance she smiled.

Here there was an outbreak of shouting from the bottom of the stairs and from the street: "Morgan! Morgan!" and a hearty round of cheers.

Kildare said: "If they stop Morgan, we may be saved, all of us. For my sake he may let us go; or for my sake he may let us burn. I can't tell what his mind will be."

Here the front door of the house was flung open and Morgan himself entered with Jimmy Green scampering behind him and running up to his shoulder the instant he came to a stand.

The greatest of all pirates had not accomplished his greatest of victories unscathed. He had a bloodstained rag tied about his head and a few smudges of burned powder did not improve the beauty of his swollen face.

He cried in his husky, battle-worn voice: "Tranquillo! Where are you, Tranquillo?"

"Keep back, all of you, and let me talk to him," said Kildare.

Then he ventured to show his head above the railing of the stairs.

A roar of anger greeted him from the buccaneers below.

"There he is!" they yelled. "He sends damn Indians to murder white men. There's Samkin in the street lying in mud that he made with his own blood."

Morgan silenced them with a shout out of his bull's throat.

"I see you, Tranquillo," he said. "And are Louis d'Or and More up there with you, along with the Indian?"

"They're here," answered Kildare.

"And the Señorita Heredia, also?"

Kildare hesitated. But she had been seen, and denial would do no good.

"She is here," he said.

Henry Morgan threw back his head and laughed.

"If you love your man," he called up, "come down to me, Ines Heredia. Come down to me, or I'll burn the lot of you like pork."

She made up her mind, instantly, and slipped through the men to the head of the stairs before Kildare caught her and snatched her back.

"Ines, are you mad?" he asked her.

"He would murder you all, Ivor," said the girl.

"Well," said More, "it would be a clean way of dying after a dirty sort of a life."

"Let her come!" shouted Morgan. "You've cheated me of her once, but your luck has run out, Tranquillo. Let her come down to me as she wants to do. There's no other bargain you can make with me! And the fire's close to the house, now. D'you hear?"

There was a great crashing close to the outer wall of the building, a roaring upward of flame, a crackling of burning wood, and almost instantly a wave of increased heat. Plainly the building on one side of the house had fallen in burning ruins, and the flames must be taking hold of the upper, wooden structure of the place where they stood.

Louis d'Or groaned: "Come at my side—we'll charge through them, Tranquillo."

"We could not any more charge through those devils than a cat could get through a pack of dogs," said Kildare. **THEN HE FELT** in a pocket and drew out his share of the treasure which had been found in the crypt of San Francisco. Among the rest, the green glimmer of four great emeralds held his eye.

"Morgan—do you see this?" he asked, and held up one of the stones between thumb and forefinger. "If you burn us, you burn more than five lives. You burn a fortune, Morgan. Are you willing to do that?"

"What is it you have?" called Morgan eagerly. "And where did you find it?"

"By prayer," said Kildare. "But look at the sample!"

He tossed the big emerald into the air and Morgan caught it in his hand. He could not help crying out with delight as he saw the beauty of the stone.

Kildare, glancing around, saw that the girl was disappearing through the door of the next room—and then Morgan was calling: "Come down, Tranquillo, and we'll talk business like a pair of friends. Where did you find this thing?"

"There are three more," said Kildare.

"Three? Is that all? There must be more!"

"What more do you wish? Any one of them would keep a man in clothes and grog the rest of his life! Four of them, Morgan! Do we talk business?"

Morgan looked down again at the emerald in his hand.

"Throw the others down," he called. "If they're worth the first, we'll make a bargain."

"You get the rest," said Kildare, "when you've sent your men back to a distance, cleared the street, and left horses in front of the building. I'll throw the other three to you the moment we're in the saddle."

"I'll see you damned first," said Morgan. "In the saddle and away?"

"Not away as fast as bullets can fly—if we try to cheat you," said Kildare.

"Suppose I make the bargain," said Morgan—"Jimmy Green, what shall I do?"

Jimmy Green, twisting to look at his master and then glancing sharply up the stairs toward Kildare, gave exactly the impression that he had shaken his head in denial.

"You see how it is?" said Morgan. "Jimmy Green won't have it. I can't let you all go. Four of these—for four lives—ay, and that leaves the girl behind. The rest of you—why, yes, you may go and be hanged. But not the girl. She stays behind!"

A wisp of smoke blew down the hall and stung the eyes of Kildare. The fire had eaten through the outer wall. The roar of it became louder, instantly.

"We'll let the fire take us first, Morgan!" shouted Kildare. "The girl goes with us!"

Then the voice of Ines Heredia sounded beside him and said: "Let him have his way; and perhaps we can cheat him!" He looked down to her and saw that she had transformed herself into a blackamoor. Black from head to foot!

25

KILDARE VERSUS MORGAN

ALL THAT BRIGHTNESS of hair was gone. She had slashed it off with a sharp knife so that it fell raggedly about her shoulders and her face; and she must have washed it with soot from the chimney and combed it out again, because it was perfectly and entirely black.

Her skin was black to the rims of the eyelids, also. From head to foot she must have bathed herself in the foul black of the soot before she put on the clothes she had found in that adjoining room.

They were what any house servant might have appeared in—short white trousers and a cheap cotton shirt, with sandals on her feet. She looked like a trivial bit of a negro lad such as might have been a servant in any house in Panama.

There were faults in the makeup, of course, considering the haste with which it had been done, and her blackness was rather streaked over the skin than put on smoothly. But the transformation was nevertheless so startling that Kildare could not believe his eyes.

He shouted down the stairs: "Morgan, it's for our lives— and we can't win away and keep her with us, at any rate. We'll take your bargain."

"Throw down the other three green beauties, then!" called Morgan.

"Not a one till you've cleared the way for us."

Morgan bellowed: "Clear back, all of you. Away from the house before the burning roof falls in on you. Trust Henry Morgan to make a bargain that will suit you all! Why, you fools, will you argue with me? Give back—and clear the street outside. You—Kilpatrick—bring four horses yonder. Do as I bid you, and on the run!"

The crowd of the buccaneers gave way grudgingly and with a good many oaths, but the authority of their chief was very great on this day, and gradually they retreated from the house. Through the open door, Kildare could see the street empty of men, and watch the four saddled horses brought.

It had grown very hot in the top story of the house. The smoke had thickened, and the crackling noise of burning wood was very close to them.

And so they started down the stairs, sword in hand, all four of them.

"I'm to run ahead and show you the way from Panama!" whispered the girl to Kildare, as she jogged down the steps in front of the rest.

"Where's the boy from?" called Morgan instantly.

"You can throw a scrap of a negro lad into the bargain, can't you?" demanded Kildare angrily. "He'll show us out from Panama."

"Where's the girl?" demanded Morgan. "Where's Ines Heredia? Unless she's turned over to me, not a man of you will—"

"Is there no shame in you, Morgan?" demanded Kildare.

"Do you want me to drag her to you with my own hands? She's hiding herself upstairs—and heaven forgive you if you find her."

"If she hid herself in the eye of a needle—still I'd find her," cried Morgan, as the shaggy-headed little blackamoor went past him down the hall.

And as the four men followed, Morgan held out his hand. The three remaining jewels were dropped into it; then Morgan ran up the stairs.

In front of the house, Kildare saw that the street was fairly cleared. A number of the curious buccaneers stood at a little distance, leaning on their muskets. Others had turned to the pillaging of the neighboring houses, and at this moment Kildare saw a Spaniard run from a doorway and try to escape across the street, while behind him appeared a buccaneer who stood in the doorway, laughing, raising his musket carelessly to his shoulder.

The gun spoke. The Spaniard leaped into the air with a scream and then fell forward on his face. He had been shot through one leg and he used the other to kick himself around in circles until the buccaneer came out and took him by the hair of the head, leaning to question him.

The screaming of the man flew into the ears of Kildare: "I have no money! I have no hidden treasure! For the mercy of God, let me live! I have nothing! I am poor!"

THE BUCCANEER MERELY laughed and seemed to enjoy a sweet music.

And Kildare told himself that he had brought this wretchedness on the city of Panama!

He remembered the long agony of the work in the galley

and the treatment of the starved galley slaves before some
of the nausea left his mind.

Then he was mounting the saddle with the rest of the
party while the noble Lady Ines of the proud family of
Heredia trotted down the street ahead of them to show
them the way. Kildare could have laughed as he got his
horse into a canter. Two or three of the buccaneers let off
their muskets into the air with shouts of anger as they saw
the Indian escaping in the midst of this escort, but all four
were at a gallop, overtaking bare-legged Lady Ines as she
scampered through the dust, when a frightful voice began
to bawl and roar from the upper window of the burning
house which they had just left.

Kildare, glancing back, saw Henry Morgan leaning from
the window cursing in a dreadful passion, while Jimmy
Green danced up and down the window sill and shook his
white-bearded face at the fugitives.

"Kill them!" yelled Henry Morgan. "Catch them and
burn them! They've cheated me! Me! They've cheated
Henry Morgan! Catch them and catch the negro lad. It's
Ines Heredia, that's worth five thousand pounds in ransom
money. Do you hear? Catch them, fools, and I'll burn them
inch by inch!"

Kildare, as his horse began to run, reached out and
caught up Ines. She jumped so that one foot was placed
on his and so she was suddenly behind his saddle; her sooty,
slender hands were strained about him.

Louis d'Or at this moment had a tremendous fall, for as
the buccaneers hastened to put in a volley before the group
should escape around the corner of the street, one of the

bullets whistled through the hair of Kildare's head; and another struck the horse of the Frenchman dead.

Padraic More pulled him up; Louis d'Or ran at the side of More with gigantic strides, hanging onto the stirrup leather.

But that was very bad. Each of the two horses had double work to do, and behind them were coming whole troops of the pirates mounted on the best that could be found in Panama and anxious to make this capture.

Five thousand pounds of ransom money? That was enough to make hearts very great indeed! And Henry Morgan himself would join the hue and cry as soon as he could get himself into a saddle.

Kildare, looking over his shoulder, saw the black, smiling face of his lady and had a silly desire to laugh; then he looked farther back to the rush of the horsemen who were coming in pursuit and his heart sickened. The horse that carried him already was beginning to labor, and Louis d'Or pulled back more and more heavily against the stirrup-leather to which he clung. This could not last long.

Kildare swung his horse to the right down an alley thick with rolling smoke and saw Louis d'Or, as he ran, clumsily leap at full speed a great burning timber that lay in the path.

They came on into an open square where he saw a number of men on horseback formed in a sort of hollow square and struggling to press through a crowd of buccaneers who beset them.

THIS WAS THE last remnant of the Spanish defense, striving only to escape from the doomed city onto the green savannahs outside it. They seemed to have a very slight chance of success because every moment saddles were being emptied by the fire of the buccaneers or by' the mighty strokes of the pirates as they pressed in hand to hand. But however slight might be the Spanish hope, it was better than that of the four with Kildare.

He cried to Padraic More: "They have to be our friends. We have to make their party ours. Ride to them, Pat! Charge through that big knot of the Brothers of the Coast!"

He had drawn his own slender sword as he spoke while Padraic More pulled out his machete and Louis d'Or unsheathed the length of his great cut-and-thrust rapier. The Indian, pushing his horse to the front, poised his spear to either cast or thrust with it. Then, four abreast, they struck the thickest knot of the buccaneers with a shout.

The surprise helped them. The flashing play of the lance and the three swords did the rest. Every bit of their steel was running blood as the buccaneers sprang right and left from this sudden destruction.

And the Spaniards, taking new heart and strength out of this unexpected reinforcement, charged in their turn and made the whole ragged, unordered mass of the pirates rush back. Kildare instantly had the girl in one of the empty saddles. Louis d'Or, springing onto another horse, became a different man at once and sent his shout through the fight.

At a trot the column worked across the remainder of the square, always keeping in good formation around the core of the party where a certain white-headed old man rode with half a dozen ladies of the town.

The rank and file of the soldiers were down or scattered; here was the last handful of the gentry of Panama trying to make good the escape of their women; and they fought like so many heroes. Many of them were wounded already; many a dead man had dropped from the ranks; but still there remained a fighting spirit that held them all together to make this final stroke for liberty.

In the confusion that followed the charge of the four, the entire column managed to surge across the square and so pass into the smoking mouth of a narrow street on the farther side.

The fumes were almost as deadly as the swords of the buccaneers. Kildare had to hold his head down and strain his breath through his teeth, but still he was choking.

But he and Louis d'Or and More, together with three of the Spaniards, made the rearguard which turned back and charged time and again into the faces of Morgan's men.

Their work was so sharp that the buccaneers began to draw back; but then Morgan himself appeared. Kildare recognized his great voice, husky as the cry of a sea-bird. Then he saw the burly pirate come charging through the fog with Jimmy Green hanging to the rear of the saddle.

A round dozen of the pirates closed at once behind their chief and gave weight to his attack. Others were ready to pour after so soon as the first impression was made on the defenders.

Kildare, looking at the befogged faces of the building left and right, where yellow heads of flame kept thrusting out of windows and roaring up the wooden sides, felt that a scene in hell might be much like this. Then, stifling and choking, he shouted to his companions to meet charge with charge. They did so. Man to man they met the mounted buccaneers.

THAT WAS AN ideal encounter for the long arm and the heavy sword of Louis d'Or. At the first shock he drove the rapier like a spear through the naked breast of a Brother of the Coast. The man dropped like a sack from his saddle and lay sizzling, unmoving, across a pair of burning timbers. Then with edge and point Louis d'Or made a havoc.

Kildare had only one purpose, and that was to get at the brutal Morgan and end this battle once for all.

In a moment he was at his man, his light-weight needle of steel engaging the heavy cutlass. Afoot or horseback, he never had fought against an overmastering fury such as that which possessed Morgan. The man was irresistible. His heavy cutlass danced like a wooden sword in his hand, and he used his breath not for fighting only, but to curse Kildare, rally his men, and shout to Lady Ines that in five minutes he would have her and then hold her to the end of his days.

The terrible strokes of Morgan's blade Kildare took on the flimsy steel of his sword with consummate skill and kept striving for an opening through which he might be able to slide the bright little gleam of steel into the throat or the breast of Morgan.

And Morgan himself, feeling the danger, raging as he found his heaviest blows turned right and left by the uncanny craft of Kildare, began to yell to his men to rescue him before he was murdered. For there was no more shame in Morgan than there was mercy.

At last, when Kildare had missed the throat of the pirate by a hair's breadth, Morgan took a new target, and with one stroke clove the head of Kildare's horse.

Down it dropped, and Ivor Kildare lay pinned beneath it,

helpless, with Morgan rushing in to finish the good work, yelling like a demon. He met at once the wide-bladed machete of Padraic More and the long rapier of Louis d'Or. They, reining their horses close to their fallen friend, now fought for his life and would not give back; and then Luis, the Indian, leaping down from his horse, helped Kildare to extricate himself from the limp weight of the fallen horse.

The smoke was less stifling, here close to the ground. The wits of Kildare recovered as he gained a breath or two of clean air. That song of the swords and the dim lightning of them above him helped him to recover, also, from the shock of the fall, and with the strength of Luis to assist, he was quickly on his feet.

A dismounted buccaneer sprang at him that instant. Kildare stabbed him through the face, and stepped quickly back to jerk his sword free from the bone of the skull in which it had lodged the point.

That backward, sudden step saved his life, for Morgan had found a chance to try a hearty stroke at the head of his enemy; the edge of the dripping blade whirred before the very tip of Kildare's nose.

He leaped in to strike a counter, catching the bridle of the horse to help himself forward. So, jumping clear of the ground, he drove the whole length of his rapier straight through the body of Henry Morgan.

26

FIGHTING CHANCE

THROUGH THE GLIMMER of fire and the gloom of smoke, the buccaneers right and left saw that stroke and uttered such howls as though the steel had pierced their own bodies.

Henry Morgan, pitching far back in the saddle, reeled and tumbled out of it, while the ape, Jimmy Green, leaped down on the prostrate body.

Here Luis the Indian, to make the fall of the buccaneer chief a certainty, ran in and struck with his spear. The blade should have gone straight through the throat of Morgan; instead, Jimmy Green by a sudden chance put himself right in the way of the stroke. He received a frightful wound, and as he screamed out in an agony, Morgan sat up and caught the bleeding body of Jimmy Green in his arms.

To the bewilderment of Kildare, the buccaneer actually staggered to his feet, shouting: "I'm only pinked through the shoulder, boys. It's a scratch. But they've murdered Jimmy Green and my luck with him! In at them—*hai*, Wilcox, Swain, Peters, Kennedy, Van Bloch, La Farge— charge 'em home! They've slaughtered poor Jimmy Green and now the devil will forget us! Charge!"

He tried to lead the way, but the rest did not follow. The

work of Kildare and Louis d'Or and More, and of three
or four of the Spaniards of the rearguard had been so hot
that the buccaneers began to prefer to go about their work
of looting Panama before it burned.

They held off, and finally a pair of them caught Morgan
by the shoulders and drew him back. He began to curse
them in a frantic voice, and all the while poor Jimmy Green
lay against the breast of his master with his skinny arms
clinging to the neck of Henry Morgan. Those arms now
lost their hold and dropped; and Kildare knew that the
strange little ape was dead. No human death could have
touched him much more.

Half strangled by the smoke, singed by the fire, he
turned, caught another horse, and soon the whole party
had broken out of the narrows of that burning street.
Behind them, to bar the way to pursuit, a house pitched
across the lane in flames with a great uproar of rising flames
and of breaking timbers.

Other buildings were staggering to a fall and went down
after the party had passed. The very soil seemed on fire
before they issued from the smoke of the town to the wide
green of the savannah, with a blue, stainless sky arched
above it.

Before them they had the battlefield with dead men
lying scattered in small heaps, in scattering groups—and in
one place a line of Spaniards lay out on the ground shoulder to shoulder, just as a volley from the buccaneers had
struck that infantry and mowed it down.

There were voices of the wounded on every side, some
groaning, sick with their wounds, others wailing for water.
Some of the poor fellows came dragging themselves

towards the party, holding out their hands for help and trailing the crimson of their blood over the trampled grass.

For already, hardly a mile behind them, they could see a small party of mounted men leaving the town and taking after them. They looked hardly greater in numbers than the Spaniards, but there would be no comparison in the fighting efficiency of the buccaneers. They might have been beaten off in the narrows of a burning street, but with an open chance to get at their game, they would pull down the Spanish as dogs might worry rabbits.

Louis d'Or drew close to Kildare, saying: "We keep Morgan's men at the same distance from us, constantly, Tranquillo; but even if we get away from them, we'll be left in the hands of the Spaniards, and they may have something to say to us, eh? How would we be able to answer their questions, Tranquillo? And once we are found out, we'll have a bit of Spanish justice!"

Kildare nodded. "We'll drift away from 'em," he said. "Are your pistols loaded? Pat, are your guns ready? We may have to do a little fighting before the Spaniards let us part from them."

MORE MERELY GRINNED and patted the big, clumsily curving butt of a horse pistol that protruded from the leather saddle holsters. With no more ado they veered away from the course of the Spaniards, taking a line to the right of the main body.

They hardly had opened up a space of ground before the white-headed commander of that lucky band called out an order and half a dozen of the gentry cantered their horses towards Kildare's band.

The leader, saluting with a wave of the hand, said: "The

noble knight, Vasco da Herta, wishes to know why you will withdraw? Our strength now is in keeping together, all of us."

Kildare answered tersely: "Tell Sir Vasco that we honor him for his wisdom and thank him for his help; but now that we're in the open, fast riding will save our skins better than any amount of numbers. We are English—two of us—and Englishmen are never safe in Spanish hands in this part of the world. We've been taught that."

"By whom?" asked the other, haughtily.

"By the Spaniards we've found," said Kildare.

The Spaniard laid his armed hand on the hilt of his sword.

"Vasco da Herta has ordered me to bring you with your will or against your will!" he declared.

"If you can afford to stop and fight while Morgan's men are coming at your heels," said Kildare, "start the game and welcome. Our pistols are loaded, and we'll promise you some empty saddles to commence with."

The emissary started at Kildare, glanced hastily about him at his tired companions—every one of them carried a wound of one sort or another—and then gritted his teeth.

"We shall see what happens!" he declared, and wheeling his horse about, galloped back to his main party with his five men following him more slowly.

Kildare kept his men at a steady trot, gradually opening more and more distance between his group and those of da Herta. He saw the messenger arrive, and saw some of the excited Spaniards handle their muskets and pistols as though they would open fire at once. But there were backward glances at the buccaneers, also, and the sight of these seemed to turn the scales in the favor of peace.

They held their original course, but Louis d'Or said to Kildare: "If they meet us again, we'll pay red for this bit of talk, Tranquillo."

"Who is Vasco da Herta?" asked Kildare of the girl.

"The oldest man in Panama—and the richest," said the girl, "and the wisest, and the most cruel. He was the judge that I had to see and bribe before you could be sent to the galleys. Otherwise, he would have had you all hanged."

"Would it be safe for us to join them?" asked Kildare.

"Every Englishman seems like a buccaneer to the people of Panama to-day," she answered. "When the wounds of these men begin to grow cold and ache; when they build their first fire in the forest and think about the homes that have been burned behind them—then they will begin to look at you, Ivor, and remember that you are an Englishman. And if they ever discover that you have been called Tranquillo—" She paused.

"Do you hear what she says?" said Kildare to his two friends.

"She talks straight as a musket shoots," said the Irishman.

But Louis d'Or said nothing at all. He had fallen into a dream as he stared, constantly, at the face of the girl. And in fact the smudging of her skin had not destroyed her beauty. It gave a strange brightness to her eyes and to her smile; and she was continually smiling. Even when she looked back at the clouds of smoke which were blowing from off the ruins of the famous city of Panama, she still could smile.

"You are not afraid?" said Kildare to her.

"Tomorrow, perhaps. But I don't think so, ever. I have enough happiness now to fill me forever."

And she touched her mouth as though to tell him that happiness had ascended that far, and this was what kept her smiling.

THEY REACHED THE top of a wooded hill and paused there. The wind had fallen, and the smooth waters of Panama Bay flamed under the westering sun. Behind them lay the pleasant green of the open savannah as far as the fumes of the dying city. Ahead of them rolled the tumult, the darkness, the broken ways or the solid jungle of the forest.

Flocks of brilliant birds, chacalacas, parrots and paraqueets, currasows and guans, were whirling over the tops of the trees; and now the bats came out with their dodging flight and wavered through the air. It would soon be night. It was night already in the forest.

"What can we do?" asked Kildare. "Speak up and make opinions!"

The Irishman said: "Steal down to the sea, wait for our chance, capture the first fishing boat that beaches, or the first periagua that we can surprise and capture. Then sail out to sea. Run aboard one of those neat little frigates that ply between Panama and the south, and so sail home to England."

Louis d'Or laughed. "Shall we man a boat with four pairs of hands around the storms of the Horn?" he asked.

"We'll put part of the Spaniards adrift," said Padraic More, "and the other part—half a dozen of them—we'll keep to help us work the ship. And that's how we'll make the voyage as trim and easy as you please."

"Vote," said Kildare.

"A big idea, not to be tried," said Louis d'Or.

"I think we could travel through the forest to the Northern Sea," said the girl.

"We'll have to try that rather than Pat's idea of the captured canoe, the frigate for a prize, and the voyage around the Horn," said Kildare. "But—have you ever traveled through the jungle, except with a hundred men to make the way safe, or cut a path through the rankness?"

She shook her head. "The vileness of it would stifle you; the heat would beat you down; and the despair would kill you, also," said Kildare.

She said: "Ivor, I have lost my father's people, my mother's fortune, and all my friends. But still I am happy. Do you think that the forest will be able to frighten me, then?"

"Forward, then," said Kildare. "We have a fighting chance to win through to England, and fighting chances are all that we're used to."

27

SURRENDER

THEY TURNED THE horses loose on the edge of the forest and entered it where a stream ran down towards the sea. The Mosquito would be able to guide them a certain amount by instinct in case the stream failed to follow the northern direction which they wanted in order to come within view of the Atlantic at last.

Silently they began that journey, stumbling over the rocks and roots at the edge of the water, and sometimes slipping into it up to their knees. It cost them half an hour to cover a half mile which was like climbing a ruined stairs. It was hard work but it was easy compared with what lay before them. And Kildare, critically watching the knees of the girl, saw that they never sagged with fatigue. She was as wiry as a boy.

They were at the end of their half mile when there was a sudden twanging of bowstrings, and a flight of arrows whirred about them. One bolt clipped past the very face of Kildare. Another actually struck and shattered on the hilt of the Frenchman's big sword.

And for one horrible moment it seemed to Kildare that an arrow had driven straight through the slender body of

Ines Heredia. It merely had whipped through the loose of her shirt.

They leaped for cover and got to it before a second volley of arrows crackled against the rocks or thudded into the tree trunks. And then a loud yelling rang through the forest all around them.

Kildare, the girl, and Luis, all found shelter behind one huge trunk.

But Luis, standing erect, was calling out in a strange tongue, talking rapidly.

A babble of voices answered, speaking from all sides, so that it was clear an Indian hunting party had hemmed them in.

"They are Cuma Indians," said the Mosquito. "But I know their tongue. I have told them that you are not Spaniards, whom they should hate, but Englishmen whom they should love."

The rest of the voices died away and a single man began to call out.

"He wants to know if you are traveling alone or if you are in advance of a large number," said Luis.

"Tell them a whole army is coming after us," said the Irishman, prone behind a big rock. "Tell them that if they put a hand on us, the army that's coming will pull down the forest over their heads."

"No," said Kildare. "Tell them the truth. In the jungle, one friendly Indian is worth a hundred blundering, starving whites. Tell them that we are four whites and yourself—all hunted by the Spanish."

He added: "Ines, try to wash the black off your face and body."

Kildare's sword was already dulled with red

She made a twist of grass obediently, and began to scrub, and he helped her. The black came off unwillingly by degrees. He rubbed sand into her hair after it had been wet, and with new scrubbings and rinsings, it began to grow bright.

Luis had finished his speech before this and been replied to. The parley still lasted through slow minutes until Luis reported: "There is a great chief talking to me. His name is Lacenta. He says that all the jungle and all the seacoast for three days' journey belongs to him. He says that the white men never have done him good and have done him much evil. But if you have presents to give him, he will take you to his village and give you guides who will take you to the Northern Sea."

The sun, unseen, had set, and the swift, tropical darkness rushed through the forest about them while Luis was speaking. Ines Heredia pressed suddenly close to Kildare, trembling.

"We can give him a pair of pistols and the powder and lead for charging them," said Kildare to Luis. "Tell him that."

The rapid voice of Luis offered the reply; there was a cheerful shout in answer.

"He agrees," said Luis.

"Will it be safe to go with them?" asked Kildare.

"Father," said Luis, "who can tell what the Cumas will do? They have been hurt many times by the white men. Perhaps they will be able to remember some of your faces, and what you have done against them in the past. And then if one of you is remembered, all of you are dead."

"Is that all you can say?" murmured Kildare.

"That is all, father."

"Do you hear, Pat? Do you hear, Louis d'Or?" asked Kildare.

"I hear," said the Frenchman. "But the blackness here is choking me like ink. Let's make the bargain and go on with them."

So that surrender—it could hardly be called anything else—was agreed on. The shout with which the Indians greeted the news showed that they regarded it as a triumph. Presently noises approached them.

Something glimmered, then a torch flared with a smoky light—another and another.

Kildare, half dazzled by that unexpected shining among the trees, gradually made out the gleam of naked bodies approaching slowly.

They were horrible things to see, the faces as red as

though the skin had been flayed from them, and the bodies black, spotted with brightest yellow in daubs and long streaks.

They wore a cloth about the loins, but that was all. They came up with arrows on the string and javelins poised.

BETWEEN A PAIR of torches there now came forward a tall Cuma Indian who carried himself with a great deal of dignity. It was a gold plate that covered his lip, and more gold pulled down the lobes of his ears.

Kildare and his friends stood in a close group as they were surrounded, and Luis said: "That is the great chief— that is Lacenta—"

Here the chief raised his hand in a sign of greeting and spoke a few words with a very lofty air, Luis translating them in this manner: "He says that he is the great-grand- son, and grandson, and son of a chief; he wants to know who is the chief among you all."

"You shall be chief," said Kildare to Louis d'Or. "You have the magnificence the Indians love."

"I haven't your wit to carry the thing off," answered the Frenchman. "You are our chief, Tranquillo. You always have been, I should say."

Here Luis, the Indian, stepped well out into the torch- light and made a little speech, after which he pointed to Kildare. Lacenta, at its close, strode up to Kildare, gripped his hand and gravely pumped it up and down; after that the party started on through the woods with the torches to guide them, the light springing up through the dark intertwining of branches to the thicker gloom of solid foliage overhead.

There was enough light and noise to start the monkeys

gibbering and swinging down through the branches to examine into the cause of this disturbance. Then the forest fell away, a series of clearings opening before them; small plantations of tobacco and of corn appeared, and thatched huts of a surprising size.

A number of other Indians came running out from these houses, and with no need of torches to light them, because once out of the thick shadow of the forest there was a moon shining which gave a clear silver light over the entire clearing of the village.

It was not like cleared land in another country. The forest which had been beaten back struggled to spring up again from the ground, and raised little hedgerows of green that presently were sprouting into big shrubs. And grass and weeds flowed in on the cultivated ground, so that there would be constant work for the women with their hoes to keep the weeds back and give the corn or tobacco a chance.

The whole throng of the villagers now poured about their war-party, a tide of coppery nakedness, prancing and leaping and howling with pleasure.

"I think we shall be safe, father," said Luis to Kildare. "I have told Lacenta the truth about you, and only the truth— that you carry a magic knife which kills a man when you point it at him, and that weapons cannot hurt you. Lacenta is very pleased and a little frightened!"

It was hardly strange that the Cuma chief was a "little frightened" about a guest who could kill men by pointing at them and who could not be injured by weapons. But that Luis had said these things in perfect good faith Kildare had no doubt, and it threw a sharp light on the entire Indian mind. Luis had seen that slender splinter of steel, in the management of Kildare, kill many a man, and perhaps he thought the touch of it was incapable of slaying unless there were magic attached.

He had seen Kildare dance through many a battle unscathed. And though he had seen Kildare wounded, also, his main impression was apparently one of invulnerability. But what if Lacenta required his guest to merely point his sword at an enemy and thereby cause the man to drop dead?

They were going up a mild ascent which brought them to the highest point of the village, where they found a great hut a hundred feet and more in length and a roof ridge at least seven yards from the ground, with the thatch running down to ten foot walls of sticks and mud.

"The war-house!" said Luis.

And now, the entrance to the hut being opened, they passed inside and found that the entire building was one great room, with loopholes the size of a man's fist cut through the walls all around the chamber, sides and ends. This was the "fort" which the fighting men would attempt to hold as a last resort in time of attack.

A fire was already burning in the middle of the floor, sending up clouds of smoke, some of which wandered out through the hole in the middle of the roof, and the rest made a mist through which gleamed the low rows of drying peppers and corncobs and all sorts of other edibles, including smoked meat. For benches, there were logs of wood.

Many hammocks strung here and there offered the only tokens of real comfort. The voices went up into the confusion of the smoke. Around the fire moved the women, all in decent white dresses which covered their bodies very modestly. They worked at the cookery and made a great rattling as they stirred, because they wore around their necks strings of teeth and shells and beads to the weight of five and twenty pounds.

Here a number of the women entered the war-house carrying among them a large trough, and staggering with the weight of it in spite of the number of their hands.

"Good!" said Luis. "It is to be a happy feast, They are bringing in the beer—and now they will soon be drunk!"

28

THE WAR-HOUSE

INES HEREDIA, SITTING on the log close to Kildare, kept her hands locked about her knees and her eyes busy with the wonders of this scene. Her bright hair, now fluffed by its shortness, shone like gold by the firelight, and all the dinginess of the soot had been scrubbed from her skin.

All of Kildare's group seemed to be very happy except Louis d'Or, who sat with his chin on his fist and gloom in his eyes, which he turned now and then and fixed rather grimly on the girl. So that Padraic More murmured at the ear of Kildare: "Louis is eating his heart out because of your lady, Tranquillo. Watch yourself!"

"Nonsense!" answered Kildare. "We are sworn brothers, Pat. He'll never turn against me."

Hunger was growing in them as they watched the cookery proceed and smelled the savor of the stews in the pots. It was a hit or miss sort of cooking. Into the pots went the flesh of the warree, peccary birds large and small, a quantity of peppers—enough to have seasoned ten times that quantity of food for a European palate—and then plantains and bananas, and the cassava, bitter and sweet, and fresh venison, and smoke-hardened meat of all sorts, and fresh fish and dried fish, together with handfuls of green herbs.

A queer humming noise rolled through the room steadily, and Kildare asked what it could be. "They are humming," said Luis. "When they are happy, the Cumas hum—or at least, all the men do. It means that later on they will want to sing."

Here several of the women began to clap their hands. At once others laid out on the beaten earth of the hut floor a number of fresh-green palm leaves, covering a long strip of the floor. Around this tablecloth the men gathered, while the women served them, placing a calabash of cold water at each man's right hand and another great dish of the stew to each half dozen of eaters.

The food had been reduced by long cooking to a sort of paste in which all the ingredients were inextricably mingled—the whole was like a soft mash of potatoes, but it contained fowl, deer, peccary, warree, cassava, and all the other ingredients of the dish hotly seasoned with peppers.

"The women are noticing me, Ivor," whispered Ines Heredia. "Do you think that it will make trouble? They're noticing me and they understand very well that I'm not a boy, as I seem to be."

"Will it make trouble?" asked Kildare. "The women understand that Ines is one of them."

"Then don't let her sit to eat with the men," said Luis. "Let her go back and wait with the other women, and they cannot make trouble at all."

She went at once, Kildare looking anxiously after her. But there was a shrill little murmuring when she came to the brown-faced Cuma women who were ranged along the sides of the great hut. Kildare saw some of those dingy hands patting and stroking the metal brightness of her hair, and he understood by this that she was being well received.

Luis, the Mosquito Indian, assured him again: "They are happy to have her. I have seen, father, that the women of many races wear different clothes or no clothes at all, but in their smiling they are always the same, and they can understand one another simply by the smiling. But this is a very great marvel!"

They were placed, all four of them, opposite Lacenta and three of his chief warriors, all men of a good deal of dignity, and at once they began to dip their hands into the central dish. It was done with a reasonable degree of decency, the two first fingers being curved to make a natural spoon.

But after every mouthful the fingers were rinsed in the calabash of water which stood beside every man, and Kildare felt no loathing whatever. For his own part, he was glad to dip his fingers in the water, both for cleanliness and to cool them, because the meat mash was steaming hot.

He found the people a prepossessing lot, a little blunt and rounded in the face and features, and in age given to gross flesh, but the children and the younger people straight-limbed, active, and graceful. Above all, they maintained an amiable expression as they talked.

LACENTA WANTED TO know a great deal about Kildare and his magic sword, which had to be drawn and admired, Lacenta wondering at the slenderness of the steel and declaring, according to the translation of Luis, that it shone by its own light, like a ray of sunshine.

When they had finished eating from the great pots, there was a store of bananas passed around, and after these everyone started drinking whole calabashes of the liquor from the trough.

The few swallows Kildare took seemed far weaker than beer, but he noticed that the effect of it was very potent. It seemed at least as strong as a double ale, though perhaps some of this was due to the heat of the atmosphere in the war-house.

As the drinking began, a message arrived from a late hunter that he had seen a whole party of armed Spaniards in the adjoining ravine, not a great distance away— so short a distance that, except for the fact that white men are incapable of movement in the forest at night, it might have seemed well to be on guard. As it was, there would be plenty of time to arm the men in the morning, and with the dawn go to plague the Spaniards and cut off their stragglers.

This news was greeted by everyone with greatest pleasure. They hated the Spaniards with a consummate passion. As for the English and other whites, they had no reason to love them except on account of the common enemy, Spain. The thought of war made the young men very brisk. They began to drink more heartily. And Lacenta himself pointed out to Kildare, with Luis always as translator, the youths of the tribe who had distinguished themselves in recent months. These had their heads shaved in token of triumph.

With the deeper drinking, the women began to move in closer to the fires and help themselves rather furtively from those eat-pots after their lords and masters had sufficed their appetites with eating. And, at the same time, the music began.

They had flutes and pan-pipes made of reed, and whistles which had been carved out of the hollow bones of the pelican and the king buzzard. Now and then someone drew a long, mournful, thundering note from a great conch shell.

The music had not continued long before a circle of the men formed and they began to dance, each man with his hands on the shoulders of his companions while he kept the time with a wriggling shake of the whole body and all the limbs.

AFTER A GOOD bit of this dancing and singing, Kildare drew back against the wall with Ines Heredia and found her a very tired girl indeed. Forthwith, he lifted her into a hammock and stood beside her. She looked up at him through half-closed eyes. "When shall I be able to sleep, Ivor?" she asked. He looked curiously around him.

Already a number of the Indians had taken to the drink in such a headlong fashion that they were overcome, and one after another they staggered towards the hammocks or were carried to them by the women, who then stood by to moisten the faces of the drunken sleepers and fan them with great palm-leaf fans.

It made a rather foolish and fantastic scene those prone sleepers, groaning as they took breath, their bodies shining with paint and with oil, and the women plying the rustling fans.

The smoke eddied in clouds; the mosquitoes sang in between; and as Kildare smiled he said: "Go to sleep as soon as you please, but I have to find Louis d'Or first. He's left the war-house—I don't know how long ago—and he may get into mischief."

"I never could trust that man," said the girl. "He has a way of looking—"

"Never doubt Louis d'Or," said Kildare, "because we've sworn ourselves to one another."

He left her, muttering to the Irishman to keep an eye on her, and went outside the great hut.

The night was amazingly brilliant, and all the villagers who were not inside the war-house were gathered about it, peering through the loopholes at the merriment within.

Kildare made the round of the house, saw the tall form of the Frenchman nowhere, and then wandered down the hill anxiously, wondering what could have become of his friend.

He reached the tall, dark frontier of the jungle without having made the discovery that he wished; and he was still standing there with his hand against the trunk of a great tree when he heard a murmuring such as comes when the wind passes through the forest, and after that he was aware that a number of figures had entered the clearing. He was astonished and rubbed his eyes to look again. But certainly the moonlight glistened on the armor of soldiers. Some two score of them were advancing softly into the clearing, but most staggering of all was his recognition of the lofty form that walked at their head.

For it was Louis d'Or.

They were surrounding the war-house. Before he could so much as shout, they were charging with a rush!

29

THE SPANIARDS AGAIN

KILDARE STARTED RUNNING, and then checked himself. There was nothing that he could do. His single hand was perfectly helpless, and he knew that everything he could conceive was useless as he saw the armored men break into the war-house from the front and from the rear.

He could understand what had happened. The devil had entered the mind of Louis d'Or and induced him to go to the Spaniards and tell them where the village lay. To the men from Panama, the possession of the village meant a great deal—food, shelter, and all the comforts until the buccaneers retired from the ruined city and the wretched remnants of the old inhabitants began to regather.

Why had Louis d'Or brought them?

It seemed to Kildare that he could see, again, the way the Frenchman had sat with his chin on his fist and his eyes lifting, now and then, towards the face of Ines Heredia.

Had not the Irishman given a warning? Had not the girl herself spoken? A singular blindness had struck the eyes and the brain of Kildare or he would have guessed everything long before.

Now, held still with hopelessness, he saw the Spaniards charge into the war-house. He had a mad desire to rush into the battle. But he could do nothing. The drunk or half-drunken Indians would be helpless. The wits of Padraic More himself were sadly addled. And the Spaniards were winning without a blow.

Kildare could tell the ease of the conquest by the noise of the outcries from the war-house. For the screaming of women was chiefly what he heard, hardly mixed by the shouting of angry men ready to fight to the last.

For long minutes that screeching lasted, and then there was quiet.

What of Ines? She must be the prize that the Spaniards would pay to Louis d'Or. What of her now?

Presently, some of the Indians began to scurry out of the war-house and run here and there, returning presently with their arms laden.

Of course they were bringing fresh supplies to the conquerors. There was no need for the Spaniards to so much as post a guard, since they held in their hands such an ample supply of hostages of the best men of the tribe, and the chief of it among the rest. They could sit at their ease, unwatchful.

It was this consideration that led Kildare gradually forward. He reached the corner of the war-house which was nearest to the jungle, and there, crouching, he was able to spy through a loophole and make out the entire scene.

It was as he had expected. Some thirty or forty of the Indians had been tied hand and foot and put under guard in a corner. Padraic More and Luis were beside the Indians, but the Lady Ines sat near the central fire, and tall Louis d'Or stood behind her with his naked sword in his hand.

The Spaniards had begun to eat, hungrily, the remains

of the feast, and drink the last of the beer. But a nucleus of them remained around the central fire.

Padraic More was at this moment picked up and dragged before the inquisitors. And the old white-haired knight, Vasco da Herta, was the one who led in the questioning.

"What is your name?"

"Padraic More."

"How long have you been in this land?"

"Not many weeks."

"Is it true that you were condemned to the galleys?"

The Irishman turned his head and gave Louis d'Or a long look.

The Frenchman bowed his head aside and said nothing.

"I was in the galley," answered More.

"Then you were one of those who rose against your commanders and murdered them and set the Negroes free?

"Answer!" shouted the old man in a rage.

"You have heard what you'll believe from Louis d'Or," said More. "Why should I talk now?"

"With you," persisted the old knight, "there was a leader who guided your hands. There was an Englishman who took an Italian name. There was that famous pirate and murderer of Christians, Tranquillo?"

MORE SHRUGGED HIS shoulders.

"Answer," shouted the old man, "or we shall find ways of making you speak!"

"If you can make me talk against my blood-brother," said Padraic More, "you'll have to turn me first into a Frenchman—like that dog I'm seeing."

He stared at Louis d'Or again.

"We know enough," said the old man, "but we wish to know where Tranquillo is now."

"I can't tell you," said More.

"You lie!" shouted the Spaniard. "Isn't it true that you sighted from the hills, to-day, the masts of his ship anchored in the mouth of the lagoon?"

Kildare started.

More, saying nothing, shrugged his shoulders.

"Isn't it true," said the old man, "that this Tranquillo has now gone down to the ship?"

Here Luis d'Or broke in to say that in fact none of them had seen the masts of the tall ship and had thought that it must have sailed straight from Panama to make the long passage around southern America, and so for the shores of England.

"Frenchman," said da Herta, "you have given us a good service, and God knows in His mercy that you are receiving a treasure for it. The lady remains in your hands, to be duly and honorably married by you, but can we trust you when you say that this Tranquillo has not gone down to the ship to rally the armed slaves and to attack us?"

"I can say that," said Louis d'Or. "He knows nothing except what I know."

"At any rate," said Vasco da Herta, "we shall make sure that the Negroes from the ship and the Englishmen who command them do nothing which we fail to observe. You, Juan Oñate—take Pedro and Jose and the three of you go down the river at once until you reach the head of the lagoon. Spy on the ship at anchor there. If the men come armed to the shore and start to advance up it, then we know you can give us warning in time. Be swift, and be vigilant."

He turned back.

"Take the heretic away," he said, "and in the morning we will have the daylight to help us devise certain ways of entertaining him, For the good of his soul—for the good of his soul! Ines Heredia, you come from an old and a noble family—but you have thrown yourself into the hands of an enemy of your people, a pirate and a traitor—"

She stood up and said: "My mother's blood was English. It is as much a part of me as that of my father. The man you call a pirate is more kind and honorable than all the best men of Panama and Porto Bello!"

Kildare heard her speaking on, and heard her voice rising, but also he saw that same Juan Oñate leave the door of the war-house with his two companions, big, formidable-looking men. Kildare heard the soft clinking of their armor as they crossed the village clearing, and he stole softly after them.

30

ANOTHER QUEST

THAT JUAN OÑATE and his two compeers, Jose and Pedro, were as good men as could be found among the Spaniards. They were fighters with gun or with sword, and they carried, as they went down the narrows of the river toward the lagoon, muskets, swords, daggers, and, many of them, body armor in the form of excellent steel cuirasses. On their heads were morions, like iron hats.

They walked abreast where they could. As the way narrowed along the edge of the water they had to move in single file, and at times the roughness of the way stretched several paces between them, man to man.

The moonlight which struck the forest sometimes slanted brightly down through the cleft above the stream, and at times it merely emphasized the depth of the shadow, contrasting with the brilliance of the moonlight that struck the tops of the trees. The Spaniards had the noise of the water to guide them even when they could not see it, for the stream rushed with a great force down the declivity always towards the sea, the huge South Sea of Balboa.

They had traveled for some time, and the head of the lagoon was not far away, appearing as a narrow edge of moon-brightened water, when Juan Oñate paused, for something appeared in the rush of the river beside him, something whirling with the current and giving out a strange flash like that of steel under the moon.

It was in fact steel; and it was the morion and the breast-plate of an armed man that Juan Oñate saw.

With arms stretched out, the body, supported by the speed of the current, kept turning and turning in slow evolutions, and then Juan Oñate saw that the face of the dead man was that of his friend Jose, that excellent warrior and good companion who could sing a song so well when once his whistle was well wetted with wine. There floated Jose, dead.

Had he slipped into the stream as he walked along, the rearmost of the three, and, knocking his head against a stone, had he been hurled down the furious current sense-less, unable to utter a single cry?

No, for as Juan Oñate, and his breathless companion Pedro beside him, stared at the corpse, they saw, clearly, the wound that had slain him—a great gash across the throat. The wound that had reached for his life also had throttled him perfectly.

His head thrown back against the force of the stream, the great gash across his throat showing clearly, Jose floated there for a moment and then was caught away by the strength of the current.

Juan Oñate turned to Pedro and murmured: "What hand could have struck poor Jose?"

"It is a miracle! Can a jaguar have followed and struck him down? Is one of the brutes behind us now?"

"A jaguar strikes with five claws, not with one," said Juan Oñate.

But both of them turned and stared into the steep, dark shadows thrown by the trees around them.

"Let us get forward into the light," murmured Pedro.

And it was then that a voice said, in very good Spanish: "Turn this way, my friends, and let me try to send you after your Jose!"

They jerked about and saw, emerging from the black of the trees, a slender man, not very tall, not more than the average height, in fact, without armor, and with only a thin-bladed sword in his hand, like a stiff ray of moonlight.

Pedro cried out: "Down with you," and tried a great side-stepping blow with his sword.

The stranger did not attempt to parry the stroke. He merely ducked under it with a quick flexion of the body.

He stepped in. His sword already was a little dim with red towards the point. When he stepped back his sword was dimmer than before, and Pedro fell dead, thrust through the heart.

At this, Juan Oñate cried out: "Magic! But my heart is clean. You cannot use magic on me! Have at you!"

He came in with a good fencing stance, and a very proper lunge such as was taught by the best fencing masters in Spain. His sword blade slithered down a soft, a yielding blade that was like the touch of a clinging hand to divert the thrust.

Juan Oñate felt that something was wrong. He tried in haste to recover his proper position of defense. He threw up his long, heavy rapier and his dagger also, to establish his guard. But between them flashed a ray of bright moonlight. A sting lighter than the sting of a wasp touched the breast of Oñate. But it was a sting that reached his heart, and he fell dead.

OVER HIM KILDARE leaned and stared for a moment. It was a great mystery, this ease with which the giant life could be plucked out of the body of strong man.

He was a practical fellow, and therefore he took a wallet from each of the dead men. Then he cast their bodies into the stream, to be hurried down to the sea. Afterwards, he followed along the course of the river towards the lagoon, and saw it broadening and brightening before him.

A moment later he could see the great ship on the water. It held up its gaunt masts and yards; its shadow was black as ink on the silver sea.

And Kildare, standing on the pure white of the beach, shouted loudly, and shouted again and again.

There was a great pause, and it seemed to him that he was crying to a picture inside a frame, a dead image—except that the ripples of darkness and of light kept traveling toward him across the lagoon. Then, suddenly, a great, obscure voice shouted from the deck of the galleon. He recognized—dimly, as though a ghost had been given speech—the voice of Bartholomew.

And a moment later men were dropping into the small skiff which was tied astern of the great ship.

Three pairs of oars strained at the water. He saw the thin shadows of them swaying and the bright flash of the water that lifted with the blades. Then they were close. Then the prow of the little boat was crushing into the sand of the beach, and next he was aware of Bartholomew himself, lisping out a cry as he bounded up the ascent of the shore;

and after Bartholomew poured the eight rowers, all crying out.

He gave them his hands.

It was strange to see the Negroes kneel in the sand and take those hands like benedictions. He gripped the horny fist of Bartholomew himself.

"I would be half way to England, by now," said Bartholomew, that honest pirate, "but the black fellows would not leave without you. They swore that you would come back to this place to meet them."

Here the Negroes leaped up and began to dance and yell. And as their black shadows lengthened and shortened on the beach, Kildare heard a great shouting begin from the decks of the Santo Spirito.

There were the fellows of the black men and the whites also.

AFTERWARDS HE WAS in the skiff with the others, and rowing out to the galleon, while the black men gave way heavily on the oars, and sang for every stroke, keeping a strong cadence. They were happy. They were so happy that they stood up to their full height as they leaned on the oars. And the water rose at the bow of the small boat and gushed down the sides with a swift gurgling noise, as of continual, rhythmic swallowing.

When they got to the ship a hundred blacks were dancing on the deck. A hundred hands were reached for Kildare.

He stood there at last under the moon and saw the signs of the great battle had been removed. There was the carpenter, and here were all the ship's crew laughing and yelling about him.

"Now hoist the sail!" cried the carpenter. "We have the

king of the Negroes! They'll be willing to make away from this place!"

Kildare then held up his hand.

He said: "Brothers, Padraic More is still alive, but he is in the hands of the Spaniards. Have you forgotten how he used an axe in the fight to win this same ship? Besides him, there is the lady I love. They are hardly an hour's march from this place. The spies they have set to watch you are dead. Who will go up with me to set on them?"

Bartholomew was a very cold-minded man, and he insisted on sitting on the bulwarks and saying to Kildare: "How many Spaniards are there?"

"Why, forty or fifty," said Kildare, honestly.

"Rabble or good men?" asked Bartholomew.

"Good fighters, every one. The bad ones were cut off by the men of Morgan."

"How armed?"

"Breastplates and morions. Muskets, swords, and everything that a man would have."

"Those damned steel breastplates," said Bartholomew, sucking his thumb, "they make a crowd of trouble. I've turned the edge of a dozen cutlasses on breastplates so that the sword turned into nothing more than a club with a blunt edge. Forty or fifty, Tranquillo? I tell you that we have only twice that many men, and the most of them are Negroes."

"They will fight, though, these Negroes," said Kildare.

"They will fight, but these dark skins will never fight like white ones," said Bartholomew.

"That is true," agreed Kildare, and was silent.

"Here," said Bartholomew, "we have a hundred thousand pounds of value in silver and gold and jewels. We have combed the hold and found a good ballasting of treasure. Enough to make us all gentlemen, after we have landed the black men in Africa and sailed home."

Kildare was silent still.

Bartholomew continued, with his toothless lisp: "You think of the Spanish girl, but you can find great ladies who'll be damned glad to have you, when they know what lines your purse."

"This girl," said Kildare, "is half English."

"Can you trust the English in her?" asked the buccaneer.

"I have crossed the Isthmus for her three times," said Kildare.

After this there was a moment of quiet, and then Bartholomew murmured: "Well, the blacks will never sail unless you consent; and we can't man the ship without them. What am I to do except to say 'Yes'?"

31

VOYAGE'S END

LOUIS D'OR COULD not sleep. He had watched the night wear on and he had seen the Spaniards, one after another, begin to slumber, but there was no peace for the big Frenchman. And he felt himself hemmed in and attacked from either side, for if he turned in one direction he found the burning eyes of Padraic More or Luis the Indian glaring at him, and if he looked another way he met the still, calm look of utter hate from Ines Heredia.

He could not sleep; he could not remain still. He had to rise and go up and down the war-house, thoughtful, grim of face.

And once he stopped near the girl to say: "Ines, do you curse me in your soul?"

She only watched him, saying nothing.

"There's nothing unfair in love or war. You've heard that," he told her.

She was still silent.

"Ines," said Louis d'Or, "the truth is that if I have done wrong, it was love for you that made me."

She continued, silently, to stare at him. And at last he realized that nothing he could say would win words from her. So he stared gloomily over the sleeping Spaniards, and then resumed his pacing back and forth.

The night had worn away for hours. The fire which had died down was replenished at last by some of the poor Cuma women who crept about the big room, only kept at a distance from the place where the Cuma hostages were kept tied hand and foot.

And immediately after the fire began to blaze up an Indian runner came into the room and fell on his knees close to the place where Lacenta the chief and the rest of his warriors were held.

The runner babbled a few words; there was a silence; and after that the newcomer said in very bad Spanish to the two sentinels who had been selected to guard the hostages: "Up the river are coming many men with long lances. They are black men, with white men to lead them along!"

That was news which easily could be interpreted. And the Frenchman cursed as he remembered how stoutly the Negroes had fought at sea against heavy odds. How would they fight now, after they had been so much longer accustomed to the use of the weapons of white men?

Vasco da Herta, however, the moment he heard the story was ready for hot action. He left three men in the war-house with orders to kill the prisoners instantly, in case the battle began to go the wrong way. The rest of his forces, including Louis d'Or, he drew out at the foot of the village, where the river crossed the clearing and plunged again into the lofty darkness of the forest.

The clearing itself was brightly lighted by the moon, and here Vasco da Herta arranged his soldiers in a semicircle facing towards the gateway which the river clove through the woods. The troops were made to lie down at ease, with loaded muskets ready for the attack, which they were to deliver with a roaring volley and then push in to engage, sword in hand. For that sort of fighting, as Louis d'Or well knew, they would have the inestimable advantage of body armor and morions. Even the leadership of Kildare, it seemed to Louis d'Or, hardly could manage to drive home a Negro attack against such advantages of position and equipment.

The long wait now began, and Louis d'Or found a wildness in his heart and in his brain while he endured the silence.

He could see the Spaniards handling their guns, now and then. And he took his own place near a fellow who wore a divided beard and an air of dignity that did not leave him even when he was lying on the ground. But the man said quietly, contemptuously: "Find another place. I cannot fight at the side of a traitor."

Louis d'Or, rising suddenly to change his position, heard old da Herta exclaim: "Dog of a Frenchman, down to the ground! Do you wish to betray us as you betrayed your own men?"

Louis d'Or, compelled, dropped down behind a bush and waited there, a burning heat in his heart. And it was immediately after this that he heard a faint sound, more like the waking of a single man than of a hundred, and finally saw the head of the Negro column march out from along the course of the river into the open And at the head of them strode Ivor Kildare, his slender sword like a twinkling bit of moonlight in his hand.

Louis d'Or gathered himself, raised—he almost had

shouted a loud warning when the voice of da Herta called out; and there followed a great roar of guns as the Spaniards poured in their volley.

The effect of it was terrible. The whole head of the Negro column was blown away—but that man of miracles, Kildare, remained standing. Almost alone, he waited for the attack of the rushing Spaniards, as they came in, sword in hand; Louis d'Or was swept along with the rush of the rest.

HE SAW THE charging line meet Kildare. He saw the slender fellow turn into a flicker of agile shadow. Two of the headlong Spaniards were down. A gap was made in their line through which the Negroes might have charged the next moment to gain a decisive advantage—and when that happened, all was lost!

Louis d'Or, with a great shout, hurled himself into the breach and attacked Kildare with his long sword with all his might, shouting.

No man could have fought better than Louis d'Or. But twice in a single moment he found the darting sword of Kildare inside his guard so that only a chance gesture with the dagger managed to parry the danger.

Louis d'Or, sweating with fear and desperation, fell back a step.

All around him he could hear the clashing of steel against steel as the Negroes valiantly fought the Spanish swordsmen. Their long-headed spears were by no means despicable weapons in such a war as this; but they could not win. Already thrusts which should have driven straight through the bodies of Spaniards were shattering against the strong steel of the breastplates. The fight could not go on forever between the skill of the trained swordsmen and the valor of the Negroes.

But as long as Kildare was there at work, the black men would not fail his leadership. And that said nothing of Bartholomew and all the other buccaneers, who were laying on with a hearty good will, shouting and cursing as they fought. But it was a losing battle, certainly—a battle which would be ended the moment that Kildare went down—for the rout of the blacks would follow.

So Louis d'Or flung himself at his enemy with a great cry. A downsweeping blow of his rapier was caught as by a hand; a long lunge was foiled, also; and then something stung his sword arm with agony. He had been run through the forearm; his rapier dropped from his hand into the rank depth of the grass and he dropped to his knees to regain it.

He was down in that matter, helpless, with the flash of Kildare's blade in his eyes, and he heard the other say: "I cannot kill you, traitor; but be sure to keep clear of me to-night!"

And the Frenchman, rising to his feet, sword in hand, saw that lithe, shadowy dancer already at work among the armored Spaniards, parrying, ducking, twisting, spinning, leaping in and out until it seemed a certainty that the man was only a silhouette operated by another force.

Louis d'Or felt the hot blood trickling down his sword arm, and went slowly back into the war-house. The three Spaniards there were shouting and cheering from the loop-holes through which they overlooked the fight in the lower village, but all that Louis d'Or could see was the bright, cold, hateful eye of the girl he loved.

And still he could not believe the thing that had

happened to him. It could not be that Kildare had spared him.

He went, deliberately, to where Padraic More was lying.

"Keep from the prisoners!" shouted one of the Spaniards, instantly on the alert.

THE FRENCHMAN, WITH a touch of his sword, cut the ropes that bound More hand and foot, saying: "Set the Indians loose! Quickly, Pat."

"My God," whispered Padraic More, "is there the blood of a man in your heart, after all?" And he caught at the dagger which Louis d'Or had dropped beside him.

All that had been seen by the Spaniards of the guard; and now a pistol boomed. It drew a loud wail of terror from the Indian women in the room; but the bullet merely knocked a hole through the wall of mud and sticks beside Louis d'Or.

At him came the three Spaniards of the guard. He parried one savage stroke, dodged a second, and then received a frightful blow across the head. The shock of the impact knocked him to his knees, but luckily the blade of the Spanish sword had turned as the blow fell, otherwise his skull would have been split like a chunk of dry wood.

Louis d'Or, still on his knees, tried to lift a feeble guard against the next attack, but most certainly he would have died if help had not come to him. A bowstring twanged; a little feather-headed arrow struck right through to the butt in the groin of the central one of the three Spaniards; and as that fellow dropped, yelling; in agony, big Padraic More came into action, howling his joy of battle.

The first weapon was the best one, so far as More was concerned. He had used the edge of the dagger to cut loose the nearest of the Indian captives; then he leaped into the fight, catching up a great war-club with a painted head. The wood of that club was tough, but it shattered to bits against the morion of the second Spaniard; the skull beneath that steel cap was crushed, nevertheless, by the sheer weight of the blow. And now Louis d'Or, getting staggering to his feet, saw the spear of Luis the Indian fly past him, the point accurately driven into the throat of the white man.

So, all in a moment, they were the masters of the war-house and of all that was in it.

They had good help, furthermore, because the Cuma hostages were no sooner free than they caught up weapons, every one, and began to do an aimless dance of exultation.

Padraic More, reaching the girl in the same first rush that had taken him through the Spaniards, had her free and on her feet at once.

Louis d'Or noted that bitterly, and then he shouted: "Outside with me, Pat! They're murdering the Negroes and Tranquillo with them!"

So they ran from the war-house and saw—all the little group of them—how desperate the plight of Kildare was.

For the Negroes, fighting very valiantly, had left a score of their number dead on the ground. Still they fought on, but more wearily, more blindly. They had blunted their spears on helmets and breastplates; the white man's magic was too strong to be overcome. Even of the buccaneers there remained standing only Bartholomew, who gasped and shouted in the thick heat of the night, and the carpenter.

But still Ivor Kildare was dancing in the thickest of the

battle like a shadow, a thing that grows small or great on the wall as the firelight flickers.

Louis d'Or, when he saw this, cried out with a great admiration: "Charge, Pat!—Tranquillo, we come!—Luis, stay here with the girl!—*Ahai! Ahai!* Tranquillo! Tranquillo!"

And he was already striking in the middle of the fight, using that sword of his which was heavy enough to carve through armor if the cunning of the point did not find its way more easily to the life.

IN A MOMENT he had broken through to the side of Kildare, and as he came closer, tall Louis d'Or was astonished by the haggard exhaustion in the face of the Englishman. Kildare, certainly, had almost danced his last step in that battle. He carried at least half a dozen wounds, and blood was running fast from all of them. He looked to Louis d'Or like a man already dead. And yet there was still the spirit in Kildare to make him cry out: "Welcome, Louis! Good lad, Pat! Now at them all together—ah ha! the Indians come in from behind—"

The Cumas had seen enough of these white men to fear them heartily. And after they were liberated from the war-house, they hung back for a moment until Lacenta, the chief, could organize them. Now, however, they made a very determined charge—against men whose backs were turned!

A sweep of arrows preceded them and did a great deal more damage than the spear-casting which followed it. That volley of arrows, coming as it did from the rear, ended the fight instantly.

Old Vasco da Herta went down at that moment with

one of the arrows stuck through the back of his head. The whole force of the Spanish soldiers wavered, broke, and ran to save their lives.

Not many of them got as far as the woods. Louis d'Or and Pat More were after them. The relentless spear of Luis the Indian marked down human prey, also, as actively as ever he could have speared fish; and Bartholomew with one mighty cutlass stroke shore through the steel ridge of a morion and the skull that was beneath it.

But the Indians were the matchless ones for the pursuit. And every Spaniard who broke away into the forest went attended by a little cluster of the red men.

That was the end, so quickly, with such a mere gesture to end what had been contested so hotly. Ivor Kildare, dropping down on one knee because suddenly he was unable to stand. He saw the darkness of the forest and the sheen of the woods mingling together; and the roar of the river was growing louder and louder, a sound that engulfed all his senses.

He began to cry out the name of Ines Heredia. But his wits were so far gone with exhaustion and effort and the loss of blood that he could not understand when she had come to him, running. He kept crying out for Ines Heredia, and yet the girl was already on her knees and in his arms.

SLOWLY THEY DRIFTED down the coast of South America, an unexciting voyage except when once they were chased for three days by a Spanish fleet. But they got away from that danger because the Santo Spirito sailed very well, even with only two masts standing; and yawing about as the leading frigate of the Spaniards drew close, Kildare and his friends put such a broadside into her that she was left standing, leaking blood through her scuppers into the sea.

Kildare himself gave orders, but he did not share in the fighting on this day. This, said Louis d'Or, was a pity, because if he had entered the fight he might have made the forty-nine battle scars which now could be counted on his body an even fifty.

They picked up, near the Horn, a tall Spanish ship which looked to be a most excellent prize; and for two days they were in sight of one another, but never once did the sea stop jumping like a nervous horse, and never once did the wind cease screaming in its highest pitch.

So they had to let that prize go, after having it securely under their guns for forty-eight hours.

This, as Bartholomew vowed, was enough of a penance to make up for every sin that they ever had committed in the past or that they ever would commit in the future.

The next day, when the sea had dropped to such a point that a boat could be launched and live in it, the tall ship was hull down in the distance, and they never were able to speak it again.

They got around the Horn quickly on one of those long slants of westerlies, and so they went up the Atlantic into warm weather.

They had the luck to pick up a Portuguese boat loaded with salt fish and salt pork, and five men aboard the little frigate all so weak and far gone with scurvy that they were glad to desert their worthless little ship.

Kildare took on board what provisions could be used and sank the useless boat; and a few days later the Portuguese were pulling and hauling and entering in the most lively manner into the work that was done on board the Santo Spirito.

They made a priceless addition without which the ship never could have been sailed home, for Kildare had made up his mind to land the Negroes in their own Africa, and in fact he did so. Into the broad mouth of a river the Santo Spirito sailed, and there were placed on the shore fifty-eight black men, all in good health.

To each man were given a pair of excellent muskets, some of the best knives, a considerable quantity of that good Peruvian cloth of which so much had been taken out of the prizes when the ship was beating about off the coast of Panama; and to every Negro were given also powder and lead, three axe-heads, two anvils, and a set of tools for a blacksmith—since two of the men had learned from the ship's smith the art of iron work—and finally whole pounds of the gaudiest beads that could be wished.

For these gifts the Negroes blessed the white men as though they had been gods from heaven, and as the Santo Spirito sailed down the river again, the black people ran along the green of the shore for more than an hour, waving, dancing, leaping, weeping. At last a strong breeze picked up the ship and sailed her rapidly away.

The Portuguese addition to the crew was very welcome from here on until at last Bristol harbor was reached and the voyage ended.

They were still in tropical seas on a night when Kildare and Ines Heredia sat in a cabin with big Padraic More, who had laid out his share of the loot from the Church of San Francisco and was telling what he would do to dispose of his money. Each jewel had to be translated by Padraic into a separate possession.

The big emerald would buy the farm; the little one would build the stone house; the two rubies should make him master of a fine stable of English runners; the flawed diamond he would give away to charity.

Padraic More, having carried on for some time in this manner, suddenly fell silent and began to shake his head.

"What's the matter now?" asked Kildare. "You have everything to make you happy so long as you live, Pat."

"I have everything," said Padraic More. "But think of him that hasn't! Think of the heart that's in poor Louis d'Or!"

He lifted his hand to call their attention, and then they could hear the regular step of a man walking the poop deck above the cabin. "Listen to him!" said Padraic More. "Now, I call it a damned thing that with all the women there are in the world, the both of you would have to fall in love with the same face."

He added, grinning: "Not that I'd want to change the face, Ines. But there's poor Louis d'Or that can't so much as look at you without turning pale. Can't you look kinder on him, Ines?"

"I cannot," she said. "He betrayed us all; he betrayed Ivor!"

"Aye, and how would a woman forgive a thing like that?" said the Irishman. "But God help poor Louis. He'll be apt to begin some bad work when he gets on shore. He'll want to have his hands full because his heart will be so empty. Well, God pity him."

"Amen," said Kildare. "Say a good word for him, Ines. Except for him we all should be lost."

"Do you think that I should try to forgive him?" she asked, her face still hard as stone, and as cold.

"I know you must before the voyage is over," said Kildare. "Today, I hope!"

"Today, then," she agreed.

"*Hai!* Wait!" called Padraic More. "I'll run and bring Louis here and have the good news."

He jumped up with a start that jarred the table, and as he slammed the door, the land, the buildings, the church, the very charity of Padraic More were all left trembling uncertainly as thoughts in the mind.

www.ingramcontent.com/pod-product-compliance
Lightning Source LLC
Chambersburg PA
CBHW030533030726
47495CB00004B/972